DEAD MAN'S BOOTS

A posse is on the trail of outlaw Jack Crow when he discovers the body of a Texas Ranger. He assumes the dead man's identity and evades his pursuers. Now, accepted as a ranger, he upholds the law: siding with homesteaders in a range war against a gang of gun-runners and the Lazy Creek ranch. In a final showdown with the renegade gang leader, Jack discovers that a dead man's boots are harder to take off than put on . . .

Books by Edwin Derek
in the Linford Western Library:

ROWDY'S RAIDERS
ROWDY'S RETURN
THE BARFLY

EDWIN DEREK

DEAD MAN'S BOOTS

Complete and Unabridged

LINFORD
Leicester

First published in Great Britain in 2005 by
Robert Hale Limited
London

First Linford Edition
published 2006
by arrangement with
Robert Hale Limited
London

The moral right of the author has been asserted

British Library CIP Data

Derek, Edwin
    Dead man's boots.—Large print ed.—
Linford western library
    1. Western stories
    2. Large type books
    I. Title
    823.9'14 [F]

    ISBN 1–84617–433–3

Published by
F. A. Thorpe (Publishing)
Anstey, Leicestershire

Set by Words & Graphics Ltd.
Anstey, Leicestershire
Printed and bound in Great Britain by
T. J. International Ltd., Padstow, Cornwall

This book is printed on acid-free paper

1

The hot and dusty trail wound ever upwards, away from the desolate Texas panhandle into a range of unnamed hills. It continued to God knows where, but Jack hoped that the trail's seemingly unending twists and turns would take him across the state line and into the territory of New Mexico. But could he get that far? The posse were too close behind for comfort and, with every stride, getting closer.

The posse were well provisioned, but more important, Jack knew they had a spare remuda of horses with them. He had no food and the steed he had 'borrowed', although game enough, was almost exhausted. He hated having to push the horse until it dropped, but he had little choice.

Jack was a Reb with a price on his head, in a land taken over by Yankee carpetbaggers. If the posse caught him, there would be no trial, just a hangman's rope. His capture rated a $1,000 reward and the poster in his pocket read: 'Wanted — Dead or Alive'. Dead would be much easier for the posse.

During the Civil War, Jack had fought in the Tennessee Militia under the command of Natham B. Forrest. General Forrest had been regarded by the leaders of both sides as one of the most able cavalry officers to serve in the Civil War, even though he had little formal military training.

However, the Tennessee Militia had been a private or partisan army, mostly funded by the wealthy Forrest who had amassed a fortune through his dealings in the slave trade. So the Militia was never part of the official Confederate Army.

After the War was over, General Forrest was accused of atrocities against captured Negroes who had served in the Yankee Army. As a result, many of the Militia's officers, including Major Jack Crow, had been excluded from the general amnesty.

In fact, a bounty was placed on Jack. At first, it was only a small amount. Nevertheless, several bounty hunters had tried to collect it. They were all dead. So far, no one had been able to match Jack's speed or his deadly accuracy. But with each victory, Jack's reputation as a gunman grew, as did the reward money for his capture.

So he had decided to drift southwards towards the Mexican border, but a few days ago, his horse had thrown a shoe. In doing so, it inadvertently began a sequence of events that was to transform Jack's life.

Of course, he had no way of knowing that at the time. So, cursing his luck, he headed to a nearby town, called Tecos. Unfortunately, its only blacksmith had been out of town working on the Lazy Creek, by far the largest ranch in that part of Texas.

So while he was waiting for the

blacksmith to return, Jack made his way to the only saloon in Tecos. It had been almost empty. Apart from Bart, the fattest bartender Jack had ever seen, a big Texan was the only other man at the bar. His battered white ten-gallon hat made him seem even taller than he actually was and he towered over Jack, who was far from being a small man.

Apart from a huge Bowie knife, unusual for its pearl handle, the huge Texan carried a massive Dragoon Colt. And he needed it. For while he and Jack enjoyed a couple of beers and were debating the likely future of Texas under the rule of the Yankees, three gunmen walked into the saloon. Clearly they had been searching for the big Texan, for the moment they saw him, they started to draw.

For a big man, the Texan was quick, but Jack was even quicker. His draw was like lightning and just as deadly. In a flash, all three gunmen were dead. Unfortunately for Jack, one of them was not really a gunman, but the son of

Brigham Boyd, the owner of the Lazy Creek.

As soon as he found out, Jack realized that Texas was no longer a safe place to be. As the blacksmith had not yet returned to reshoe his horse, Jack 'borrowed' one of the dead gunmen's horses, tethered outside the saloon. Then he hit the trail for Mexico.

Since then, no doubt spurred on by the promise of additional reward money by Brigham Boyd, a posse had relentlessly followed him and almost caught him too, but he had hidden in a clump of cottonwoods and watched them ride by.

But in doing so, the posse had got between Jack and the Mexican border. So he had been forced to take a little used hill trail, which he hoped, rather than knew, ran west into the wilderness of the New Mexican Territories. His move had caught the posse by surprise and it was several hours before they relocated his trail. But, mounted on an exhausted horse, Jack's advantage could only be temporary. Perhaps he should not have helped the big Texan, but it had never been his way to stand aside when a fellow Reb needed help.

Again, he spurred his tired horse onwards. Always climbing, the trail continued to twist and turn through the steep-sided hills. As the day wore on, it became hotter and he could feel his horse begin to falter. So, in spite of the danger behind him, he reined in the exhausted beast and dismounted. Jack had been brought up amongst horses and could not push this one any further. Instead, he inverted his hat and poured the last of the water in the canteen into it, then gave it to the horse.

After it had finished drinking, Jack began to lead it slowly up the trail, hoping to reach its summit and remount before the posse caught up with them. However, he never reached the summit, he didn't have to do so. If fate had been unfair to him since the end of the Civil War, then Providence was about to intervene in a most unexpected manner. His outlaw life was about to end and a new one begin.

The buzzards wheeling high over the trail just ahead should have alerted him. But he was hungry, desperately tired and his feet hurt. His old cavalry boots were made for riding, not walking. Furthermore, his attention was focused on the trail behind him as he strained to catch the first sounds of the pursuing posse. So, as he rounded the next bend, he was quite unprepared for the scene of carnage in front of him. But, at first, he only saw the overturned stagecoach.

Slewed sideways, it almost blocked the trail. There were no traces of its horses but there was a woman passenger inside it. Like the stagecoach, she wasn't going anywhere. She was dead, scalped by whoever had attacked the stage. Exactly the same fate had befallen the guard and driver; their bodies lay unmoving on the ground on the other side of the stage.

The massacre had not long taken

place, for when Jack examined the bodies they were still warm. But the attack had not been carried out by any Indian tribe or sub-tribe he had ever encountered. Indeed, he was doubtful that the raid had been carried out by Indians.

Jack Crow was not the name given to him at birth. While he was still little more than a toddler, his real parents had tried to cross the badlands of the Indian Territories. Very unwisely, they had decided not to go in a wagon train but to go alone and unescorted.

They had been killed by a marauding band of Apaches, but these savages had been intercepted and killed by Crow Indians who took Jack into their tribe. Thirteen years later, a preacher realized that Jack was not an Indian. The Crow, perhaps the nomadic warrior tribe most friendly to white settlers, readily agreed for the preacher to take him back. The preacher then christened him Jack Crow.

Because of his Indian upbringing,

Jack looked at the scalping of the woman in disbelief. For most Indians, scalping was simply a matter of taking coup. An honourable way for a brave or chief to show how many enemy braves he had killed in battle. Indian women took no part in such battles, their place being very much the lodges, raising children, preparing and cooking food. So there was no honour to be gained in taking the scalp of a woman, even if she was white.

Then there was the way the supposed coups had been taken. The whole of the scalp had been removed from the victims. As far as Jack was aware, Indians only normally removed the hair which grew over the forehead.

But the posse was getting ever nearer, so there was no time to try and solve the puzzle. Instead, he searched the driver and guard in the vague hope of finding something to help him. But he found nothing of interest. Had he searched the woman, he would have discovered her true identity.

But his sense of decency and honour would not permit him so to do. Instead, he searched a fourth body, partially hidden in a gully. It was a man of roughly the same age, hair colour and appearance as Jack. He had been killed by a single shot to the forehead. Oddly, he had not been scalped, nor had his Navy Colt been removed from where it lay beside the body. Again, there was no time to try and solve the puzzle.

Jack searched the body and found a wallet. From some of the documents in it, he discovered that the dead man had been called Bob McAllen. Recently enrolled into the Texas Rangers, he had been on his way to Fort Caddo. His wallet also contained instructions to report to a Captain Jim Ward. So it seemed unlikely that anybody in Fort Caddo had met the dead man.

As Jack looked at the dead Ranger a wild idea began to fill his mind. Only two people could positively identify him as Jack Crow. One was Bart, the obese bartender in Tecos. The other was the big Texan he had aided. He was either long gone or already dead at the hands of the posse.

Of course, it was possible that Bart had given a too accurate description for Jack to get away with the deception he was planning. Yet the more he looked at the dead Ranger, the more he favoured the idea. Indeed, almost anything would be better than trying to outrun the posse mounted on the fresher horses of their remuda.

There was, however, one major problem in swapping identities. The Ranger wore new and expensively patterned boots. Jack's old cavalry boots were badly worn, a relic from his days with the Tennessee Militia.

There was no getting away from it. To have any chance of getting away with the impersonation, Jack had to exchange clothes with the dead Ranger. But would McAllen's boots fit him?

Stripping the dead man was much harder and took far longer than Jack had expected. But taking off his own clothes and changing in to those of the dead man took just a few seconds. He also ensured that anyone searching McAllen's body would easily discover Jack's Wanted poster. Fortunately, the poster didn't contain his picture and its description of Jack was broad enough to fit the dead Ranger.

Unfortunately, the macabre task of putting Jack's old clothes on to the dead man turned out to be quite difficult. Although they were identical in height, McAllen was a little more heavily built than Jack. So Jack's old clothes were a tight fit on him. Yet once on, their tightness was hardly noticeable.

Jack's old boots slid easily on to the Ranger's feet. But would McAllen's fancy boots fit Jack? Surprisingly, taking in to account the dead man's heavier build, his boots were a size too small. But Jack managed to get them on.

That Jack was unable to walk far in them was not a problem. Walking more than a few paces was detested by virtually all cowboys, especially those who hailed from Texas. Cowboys rode everywhere, farmers and homesteaders walked, was a well known Texas saying.

Jack then had to haul the dead body back on to the trail. This further hurt his already sore feet. Next, he retrieved the dead man's empty Navy Colt, reloaded it, fired one shot into the air, then returned the handgun to the dead man. Then he fired another shot with his own, larger, Army Colt which, together with his gunbelt and ammunition were the only things of his own he retained.

Eventually, breathing heavily and sweating profusely, Jack sat down in the shade of the stagecoach and waited for the posse to arrive.

2

As the posse approached Jack hailed them like long lost friends, as he assumed any Ranger would have done. There were nine riders in all, but no sign of their remuda of spare horses. As three of the posse members dismounted, the others fanned out to cut off any possible escape. Two of the deputies who had dismounted began to examine the bodies, while the third drew his six-gun and slowly approached Jack.

'I'm Sheriff Hicks. Suppose you tell me who you are and what the devil happened here?'

'Bob McAllen of the Texas Rangers,' lied Jack as convincingly as he could.

'Can't say I've heard mention of that name and I know most of the Rangers around here.'

'That's not surprising, Sheriff. I'm

new to the area. Here's my papers,' said Jack.

He slowly reached into his pocket and handed the wallet he had taken from the real Bob McAllen to the sheriff, who shifted his six-gun to his left hand, then took the wallet.

'Over here, Walt!' the lawman called to one of the deputies searching the bodies. 'Keep a close watch on our friend here, while I go through his papers. Shoot him if he so much as moves a foot.'

Slowly the sheriff examined the documents. Jack stood motionless, keeping his right hand well away from his six-gun. He did not want to give the trigger-happy deputy the slightest excuse to gun him down.

'These papers seem in order,' said the sheriff at last, returning the wallet to Jack.

Jack began to relax. The sweat on his brow was not entirely due to the hot sun. But he relaxed too soon. Just when he thought he had got away with the deception, the lawman transferred his six-gun back to his right hand, then pointed it directly at Jack.

'So what happened here?' he asked menacingly.

'Well, I can only tell part of it,' replied Jack.

'Part is better than nothing,' replied the sheriff. 'But choose your words with care. I've still a mind to string you up, whether you're a Ranger or not.'

Jack launched on the story he had been rehearsing while he waited for the posse to arrive.

'Last night my fool horse stumbled and threw me. Must have hit my head as I fell, because when I came round the animal was gone. With him went my rifle and most of my water supply. So I cut across the hills until I came across this trail. Been walking along it for a couple of hours when I came across this stage. It was exactly as you see it now, all the people on it were already dead.'

'Sheriff, come over here!'

Jack's none-too-convincing story was

interrupted by Walt. He had found the Wanted poster Jack had planted on the body of the real Bob McAllen.

The sheriff studied the poster carefully.

'I ain't too convinced by your story,' he said doubtfully. 'But I guess the description just about fits the dead man. And the name on the poster is the name he gave to Bart. But if it's the man we've been chasing, what's he doing mixed up in a stage holdup and why ain't he scalped, like the others? Unless you can explain that to me, Ranger, to be sure we get our man, I guess we're going to have to hang you after all.'

'I shot him,' said Jack calmly.

'Go on,' said the sheriff.

'As I said, all the folks on the stage were dead. But the man you seem so interested in wasn't one of them. Just after I arrived, he came galloping up the trail as if the devil was chasing him.'

'Or a posse,' mused Sheriff Hicks.

'Mean cuss he was too. Although his

horse was about done in, he refused to stay and help. When I tried to stop him riding off, he went for his gun. But I guess he wasn't as good as he thought he was.'

'You must be damned quick,' growled Sheriff Hicks. 'The man you say you outdrew was Jack Crow, an outlaw who has killed a dozen or more in gunfights. But we're after him because he and his side-kick shot three good men in my town. The other man got clean away, but we've been on Crow's trail ever since.'

'Quick he may have been, but you've got to hit what you're aiming at. He missed, I didn't.'

Walt, the sheriff's senior deputy, checked the real Bob McAllen's Navy Colt. Smiling, he handed his canteen to Jack who accepted it gratefully.

'One shot recently fired,' Walt said. 'I guess that confirms your story, Ranger, and we can get back home.'

However, Sheriff Hicks was still not completely satisfied. But further questioning was prevented by the arrival of the remuda. Apart from ten spare horses, there were several pack mules and burros carrying food and water. It had been these animals which had caused the remuda to fall behind the posse.

The remuda was led by an unarmed lad. Acting as wrangler, he looked little more than sixteen years old. His face paled as he saw the dead bodies. Jack guessed they were the first the boy had seen. So he was surprised when Sheriff Hicks made the lad drag the bodies into the gully and cover them with stones. It was no job for a boy, so Jack went over and helped him while Walt and the sheriff unceremoniously draped the body of the real Bob McAllen over a pack-mule.

The rest of the posse helped themselves to food, even sharing some of it with Jack, whom they seemed to accept as Bob McAllen. But the boy declined to eat; he only just avoided being sick.

After the meal, the posse changed horses and Jack was offered the spare mount. Much to his relief, he was not destined to return to Tecos. As the posse members and the remuda turned back, Sheriff Hicks laid a restraining hand on Jack's horse, then called for Walt and another deputy to remain behind.

'It ain't that I'm doubting your story,' he said to Jack, 'but I've got to take Crow's body to Fort Caddo and get the federal judge to certify him dead before my boys can get their reward. So as you're going to join the Rangers there, it's best you come with us. You wouldn't want to be on your own if you ran into the Indians who attacked the stage, would you?'

Put like that, Jack had to agree. He had hoped all the posse would return to Tecos, leaving him free to head over the border, where he would have dropped his impersonation of the dead Ranger. Now he had to take the chance that no one in Fort Caddo had met the real Bob McAllen. He had never been in this part of Texas, so it never occurred to him that he might meet someone who had recently known him as Jack Crow.

Slowed down by the pack-mule, it was an hour after dawn before they reached Fort Caddo. It was nothing more than a settlement, although its centre had once been a fort or stockade. Its general appearance belied its name. The Caddo were a small tribe of Indians who mostly lived in the south-east of Texas. Although their homeland was many days ride away, Jack had assumed the town had been named after them. Yet there were no signs of any Indian ancestry. The main street leading to the old fort was lined by wooden, American style buildings. However, all the alleyways were lined by white-painted, adobe houses and cantinas of Mexican origin.

They rode on to the old fort which had only one entrance. Inside it was a large rectangular courtyard. To the right was a large stable and blacksmith's. Facing them, on the opposite side of the courtyard, was a tatty, three-storey, saloon-cum-dance-hall.

But the sheriff rode straight to the far end of the courtyard and dismounted in front of Fort Caddo's only hotel. Unlike the much larger and dilapidated saloon, the hotel was in immaculate condition, having been recently repainted. Walt led Jack into it and ordered breakfast, while Hicks and the other deputy took the body of the real McAllen to the Rangers' office, which was situated on the corner of the courtyard.

After breakfast, a very average meal, but eaten with some relish by the half-starved Jack, they too, made their way to the Rangers' office. Fort Caddo, an isolated and half-forgotten settlement, no longer had its own sheriff. Instead, waiting for them was the notorious circuit judge, Marmaduke Pulse. However, the rather portly man of the law was much better known as Hanging Judge Bin, a name which he did his best to live up to.

With him was the last man on earth Jack expected to see, the big Texan from the shootout in the Tecos saloon. In the confines of the office, he seemed even taller and towered over the portly judge. The Texan was still wearing his battered old ten-gallon hat and carrying the big pearl-handled Bowie knife.

But who was he? Jack's heart sank. It seemed his impersonation of McAllen was about to be revealed. With Sheriff Hicks and the other deputy in front of him and Walt behind him, there was no way he could escape. Besides, he had no wish to draw against the likeable Texan.

Yet the big man gave no sign of recognition, nor did Sheriff Hicks identify the Texan as the other man in the shoot-out. Yet Bart, the bartender, must have given Hicks a description of the massive Texan. Besides, how many people carried a knife like the very unusual pearl-handled Bowie?

Nothing seemed to make sense. As if they had never met, the Texan asked

Jack for McAllen's papers and read them carefully. Then he passed them to the judge who also studied them intently. Time seemed to stand still. Jack hardly dared breathe. Expected to be found out at any second, his right hand instinctively moved towards his six-gun. Yet nothing happened.

'These papers seem in order,' said Judge Bin, breaking the spell.

Jack could hardly believe his ears. What was going on?

'So you can confirm that this man is Bob McAllen? asked Sheriff Hicks.

'Who else would you suppose him to be?' replied Judge Bin, cleverly avoiding answering the question.

'He could be the outlaw we were chasing.'

'Jack Crow?' said the judge, brilliantly feigning surprise. 'What makes you say that?'

'He could have met the real Bob McAllen on the trail and shot him, Crow is a noted fast gun.'

'Was, you mean,' interrupted the judge.

'But he would have had to change clothes with the dead man and then wait for you by the stagecoach. Sure take a man with a lot of sand in his craw to do that,' said the big Texan, staring hard at Jack.

The sweat on Jack's back made his shirt cling to him. Yet the day was not yet hot.

'Don't seem likely,' said the judge thoughtfully. 'If Crow had shot McAllen, why didn't he just change clothes and ride away? Why come here and risk being discovered? He must have known we were bound to check up on him.'

Jack's hand settled on his gun belt. Had Judge Bin just been toying with him? Was this the moment the judge was going to denounce Jack?

'What about his boots?' interjected the big Texan.

Jack breathed more easily. The moment of danger seemed to have passed.

'Boots? I don't understand?' said a puzzled Sheriff Hicks.

'When you first came in you gave us the description of your killer and told us the bartender at Tecos said that Crow was wearing old cavalry boots. If this man here is Crow, he would have changed boots with the dead man. For both men to be near enough the same size to be able to do that seems a mite unlikely,' said the big Texan.

'Unlikely, but not impossible,' said the judge thoughtfully. 'Sheriff, if you insist, I'll send a man to San Antonio and get him to bring back somebody who knew the real Bob McAllen. Unfortunately, that may take several weeks. Until then,' the judge pointed at Jack, 'this man will have to remain here under guard.'

Sheriff Hicks began to fidget. He didn't like the way the conversation was going. He had no idea that Judge Bin was bluffing. The last thing in the world the judge wanted to do was to contact San Antonio and draw attention to one of the last companies of Rangers still operating in Texas.

Aware of the Rangers' strong and active support for the Confederacy during the Civil War, the new Yankee masters of Texas were in the process of disbanding them. But the Rangers operated in small, semi-independent bands called companies, so each company had to receive formal notification.

Situated on the far side of the panhandle near the Texas border with the territory of New Mexico and only a few days' ride from Mexico, Fort Caddo was about as remote as it was possible to get in Texas. The new authorities had not got round to disbanding its Rangers, but the judge knew they were operating on borrowed time.

However, the sheriff knew nothing of the Rangers' problems. His only concern was to get the McAllen situation resolved quickly. He was only too aware that his deputies were already convinced that the dead man was Jack Crow and would have told his boss, Brigham Boyd.

The powerful boss of the Lazy Creek was not noted for his patience and without his support the sheriff knew he could not get re-elected. Besides, his deputies would be expecting their share of the reward money. So the lawman came to a quick decision, the one the judge had intended him to make.

'I guess you're right,' said the sheriff. 'If I had swapped clothes and boots with a dead Ranger, I would have high-tailed it for the border. I sure as hell wouldn't have waited for the posse chasing me.'

'As long as you're sure,' said the judge, smiling knowingly at the big Texan, 'I guess we can go to the bank and sort out the claim for reward money.'

An hour later, Sheriff Hicks, Walt, the other deputy, the pack-mule and the horse Jack had borrowed, left town. Feeling more than a little satisfied with the way things had turned out, the judge returned to the office where Jack was being guarded by the big Texan.

Much to his surprise, Jack had discovered that the Texan was Jim Ward, captain of what still remained of Fort Caddo's company of Rangers. The man to whom the real Bob McAllen was supposed to report.

'So, what happens now?' asked Jack, bewildered by what had just happened.

'I guess the judge will use a little Texas-style common sense,' replied Jim.

'Certainly,' said Judge Bin.

'I don't understand,' said Jack.

'When the facts don't fit the truth, we Texans sometimes find that it can be more prudent to re-examine the truth to see if it can be made to fit the facts,' said Judge Bin, still smiling.

Rather than provide an answer to Jack's question, the judge's words only served to further confuse Jack. Seeing the puzzled look on Jack's face, the judge continued:

'Fact one, a dead man has been brought in and identified by the sheriff of Tecos as the wanted outlaw, Jack Crow. Fact two, using my authority as circuit judge, I have authorized the payment of the reward offered for the capture of Crow.'

'Fact three,' interrupted Jim. 'You saved my life in Tecos risking your own to save somebody you had only just met. Not the action you would expect from a wanted killer.'

'But just what you would expect from a fellow Ranger,' said the judge.

'Fact four,' continued Jim, 'you turn up again with the lawman from Tecos, claiming you shot Crow.'

'Fact five and the clinching factor,' said the judge, 'instead of claiming the reward, you produce documentation to say you are the Ranger we have been expecting to join us.'

'So welcome to Fort Caddo, Ranger,' said Jim looking directly at Jack. You've made a good start, but I will expect you to keep it up and not let the judge down. I'd be forced to track anybody down who did and I'd hate to have to use my old Bowie knife on anybody who saved my life.

Do you understand me, Bob?'

It took Jack a second to respond to his new name.

'Perfectly. I'll do my best not to let the Rangers down. Here's my hand on it.'

Jim gladly shook the proffered hand and the bargain was sealed.

3

It was almost noon. Judge Bin led the way into the busy saloon. However, the judge had his own table which was always reserved for him. A cold lunch and drinks, all paid for by the hanging judge, were served by two very attentive saloon girls.

In spite of his fearsome name, the judge proved to be a jovial companion. For the first time in many months, Jack began to relax and asked the judge about his unusual nicknames.

'Well, a lot of know nothing, do-gooders back East think my sentences are far too harsh. That isn't true. Round here, there's not always time for what they call due process of the law, with fancy courts full of pretty lawyers. If a man's guilty we hang him quick. But I've studied books and travelled far and wide. I think very carefully about the bad things which might happen if the prisoner is let off, so no man gets hanged in my court who don't deserve it.'

'Tell him why you changed from Pulse to Bin,' said Jim, knowing only too well that one of the judge's oldest and most repeated stories was sure to follow.

'As I said,' continued the judge, smiling happily, 'I'm a well-read man. Pulse is just a fancy name for a good old bean. But I'm not an impulsive man.' The judge laid heavy emphasis on the middle syllable and paused for effect before continuing. 'But as I just said, I've Bin almost everywhere.'

The judge laughed uproariously at his old and not that funny joke, then turned to Jim.

'Better get our new man fixed up with some decent digs. Put the bill on my account and I'll take the money out of Bob's next month's pay.'

It again took a second for Jack to react to his new name, then he nodded his head in agreement.

'My Rosa's got a nice little spare room,' said Jim. 'She won't overcharge you and she's the best cook in Fort Caddo, if I do say so myself.'

On the way to Rosa's house, Jim gave Bob, as Jack now tried hard to think of himself, a rundown of the major problems facing the Fort Caddo Rangers.

'Rustling, gun-running and the new US Cavalry, not necessarily in that order,' said Jim with a wry smile.

'The US Cavalry, I don't understand?'

'The Cavalry is now responsible for dealing with the Indians, or hostiles as the troopers call them. But their officers are mostly fresh out of the Academy at Westpoint. The only Indians these kids have seen are the tame ones back East. Out here we got all kinds of red devils. Different sub-tribes of Apache like the Apache-Kiowa and the Comanche. The Cavalry go chasing after them, flags flying and bugles blowing. All they caught so far is a lot of arrows in the back. Yet we Rangers who have fought all the different Indian tribes for most of our lives ain't allowed to help, not even as scouts,' said Jim bitterly.

'What about the rustling and gun-running?'

'Same source, the Lazy Creek,' replied Jim as he pointed towards Rosa's little white adobe house. Jack was glad to see it, the fancy-patterned boots he'd taken from the real Bob McAllen were made for riding, not walking. Being a size too small didn't help either. He asked more questions just to keep his mind off his aching feet.

'Why should a big outfit like the Lazy Creek go in for rustling and gun-running?'

'Haven't got a clue, Bob. That's what I was doing in Tecos. Trying to dig up any information I could about the activities of the Lazy Creek. The bartender, Bart is one of our under-cover men. He gave Sheriff Hicks a false description of me, which is why

Hicks didn't recognize me. You can trust Bart but not Hicks. That lawman only does what the Lazy Creek's boss, Brigham Boyd, tells him to do.'

They eventually reached Rosa's adobe house. Clearly Rosa was far more than just Jim's landlady, for she embraced him passionately. Jack was still having difficulty in thinking of himself as Bob McAllen, which made him a little awkward over the introductions. Fortunately, Rosa interpreted his hesitation as shyness. Jim had to leave as soon as he had introduced Bob, muttering as he did so something about a Ranger's work never being done.

Dark-haired and typically Mexican in appearance, Rosa was about thirty, a little on the plump side, but good-looking. She had a strong outgoing personality and was not afraid to speak her mind. She immediately made it clear that Bob's appearance and the state of his clothes were not acceptable.

'You stink, I think,' she said wrinkling her nose in distaste. But the twinkle in her eye belied the tone of her voice.

But she was right. Bob had to admit he positively reeked of sweat, trail dust and of being too near a horse for a long time. Although the clothes he had changed into were a little newer, they were no fresher than his old outlaw ones.

Within the hour, Rosa had a steaming bath-tub ready for him. He stripped and, to the great relief of his aching feet, soaked himself in its soapy water. He had just begun to relax when Rosa suddenly appeared. In spite of all Bob's loud protests, she proceeded to scrub his back, threatening to empty out the bath-water if he didn't stop complaining.

Covered only in embarrassment, Bob could only cower under the soapy water and wait for Rosa to finish. However, when at last she completed the job, she removed all his smelly clothes, leaving only a very small towel which covered far too little of his naked body for Bob's ease of mind.

Gingerly, he got out of the bath-tub.

Barely stopping to dry himself, Bob wrapped the tiny towel around him as best he could and slowly opened the door. Rosa was nowhere in sight, so he made a dash to the comparative safety of the spare bedroom. Thankfully, there was nobody there and Rosa had drawn the curtains. But, except for his boots, or rather the boots he had taken off the body of the real Bob McAllen, there was no sign of his clothes. So he climbed into bed. He had no intention of falling asleep, for it was only mid-afternoon. However, he had been on the run for weeks, long before he had ridden into Tecos, and had ridden all through last night with Sheriff Hicks, Walt and the other deputy. So when, five minutes later, Rosa popped her head round the door, he was fast asleep.

4

A week later, the newest addition to the company of the Fort Caddo Rangers rode slowly out of the settlement on a little mustang loaned to him by Rosa. As it was barely dawn, the streets were almost deserted, but anyone looking at the former outlaw would hardly have recognized him.

Only his expensive boots had survived Rosa's purge. As they had belonged to the real Bob McAllen, they were, really, *dead man's boots*. The clothes he now wore had been obtained from Rosa's younger brother. They were well-worn and far from a good fit, but at least they were clean.

It was his first mission and Bob, as Jack had now begun to think of himself, was somewhat surprised and apprehensive. He was surprised to be allocated a job away from the close scrutiny of Jim

Ward so soon, apprehensive because he now represented the law from which he had so often run.

Bob rode south until noon, then turned east across the panhandle along a little-used trail. Far to the north, he could just make out the hills through which he had been chased by Sheriff Hicks and his posse. But he had to put those days behind him if he wanted to become a Ranger.

But did he really want to become a Ranger, or just impersonate one until it was safe to move on? He wasn't sure. But he had given his word and shaken hands on the deal. So he put aside any thoughts of making a dash to the Mexican border until he had successfully completed the mission he had been given.

Rosa's little mustang began to tire, so he rested it for a while. Bob sighed as he remembered the many fine horses he used in the Tennessee Militia, any one of which would suit him better than this little mustang. But on a Ranger's salary of one dollar and a quarter a day, it would be a long time before he could afford the sort of horse he really needed.

But in other ways he was well off. He still had his old Army Colt, but the carbine in his saddle scabbard was the new and still rare Winchester .44. Like the superb Henry rifle it was intended to replace, the Winchester was a breech-loading repeater which could carry thirteen bullets per magazine. But its revolutionary, factory-made, metallic cartridge was far more powerful and reliable than the 'roll your own' percussion bullets, making every other shoulder weapon obsolete.

The Winchester .44, together with its new ammunition and a shotgun, had been provided by Jim Ward. This was a generous gesture as Rangers were normally required to provide their own guns, ammunition and horse.

Slowed down by the lack of stamina of Rosa's mustang, it took Bob two days to reach his destination, the small town of Cottonwood. Situated in the heart of the arid Texas panhandle, Cottonwood was hardly bigger than a settlement. Yet although it consisted of no more than twenty wooden buildings and a population of just less than one hundred, the little town was entitled to a sheriff. He was Hal Young and it was to his office that Bob slowly made his way.

But habits formed when on the run die hard. Instinctively, Bob looked for escape routes out of the small town. However, Cottonwood's few buildings were not arranged neatly along a main street. Instead, they were spread-eagled in an untidy circle with no roads between them. Fortunately, the ground was usually baked rock-hard by the hot Texas sun, so the absence of proper connecting streets and sidewalks was not normally a problem.

Yet, in spite of its lack of size, Cottonwood was a lively and busy place. Apart from the usual livery stable and general store, it had a small church and three large saloons. This was an apt reflection on the character of the most frequent visitors to the town: cowboys or gunmen seeking employment on the huge Lazy Creek.

In fact, it was one of these gunmen, the leader of a small but notorious gang of renegades, who was the main reason for Bob's visit. Hal Young had requested help from the Rangers in arresting him. The gunman was Daag Ward, half-brother of Jim Ward. Daag was as mean and treacherous as the captain of the Fort Caddo Rangers was honest and loyal.

Nevertheless, Judge Bin had said that, blood being thicker than water, he did not want to send Jim after his own kin, so he ordered Bob to do the job. The judge's real reason was that he believed that Daag was faster on the draw than Jim and would not hesitate to kill him in the event of a shoot-out.

However, bearing in mind the task might take him near to the Mexican border, Bob thought the judge was testing his loyalty. Bob's suspicions had been further aroused when the judge had also instructed him to question at least some of the homesteaders situated near the Rio Grande to see if any of them knew anything about the Lazy Creek's alleged gun-running activities.

Although he was now an accredited Ranger, walking voluntarily into any sheriff's office still gave Bob a distinctly uncomfortable feeling. But he need not have been concerned as he was given an enthusiastic welcome by Hal Young, who seemed quite relieved to see him.

In spite of his name, the sheriff was a veteran of the Texas War of Independence and also a former Ranger. But Hal Young had no illusions about the effect his advancing years was beginning to have on his prowess with a six-gun, as he freely admitted to Bob.

'Was a time when I could match most with a handgun but no longer. Until recently, the worst I've had to deal with was the odd drunken cowboy on a Saturday night.'

'But Cottonwood is pretty isolated, didn't you have any problems with the Indians?' asked Bob.

'Some. But not for some time. At first the Apaches were the main problem. Then Comanche hunting-parties started to raid the nearby homesteads. It seems at least some of the Apaches took exception to the Comanches' raiding-parties and hostilities broke out between them. As a result, they mostly left us alone, although a few of the more isolated homesteads were attacked.'

'What happened to them?' asked Bob.

'Gobbled up by the Lazy Creek. Brigham Boyd then began to hire gunmen. He said it was to protect his ranch. May be true, but I have my doubts.'

'Why?' asked Bob.

'Because he keeps on hiring more and more gunmen. He already has far more than he needs just to guard his own ranch. Yet another bunch of gunmen hit town last week. They are nothing but scum and their leader, Daag Ward, is the worst of the lot. He's openly bragging that Brad Clark, top hand at the Lazy Creek, will be here in a few days to hire them. Since Boyd is picking up all the gang's bar bills and they seem intent on staying out of trouble, I believe him.'

With that, Hal Young left to begin his afternoon patrol, leaving Bob to mind the office. Although the patrol didn't take long, Hal returned with the news that Cottonwood's saloon-owners would cover any bills Bob incurred during his stay in their town, just so long as he got rid of Daag Ward. However, during his patrol, Hal had established that the renegade and his gang were not in town but were expected back sometime tomorrow.

So Bob stabled Rosa's mustang and grabbed a bite to eat at one of the saloons. Unusually, the saloon boasted a balcony with a large parapet, over which skimpily dressed women would occasionally peer. Although there were several gunmen hanging around, none of these girls came down the balcony stairs to ply their trade. As Hal had said that none of the gunmen currently in town appeared on any of his Wanted posters, Bob ignored them and the rest of the day slipped peacefully away.

However, there was always the possibility that Daag and his gang might return unexpectedly during the night. Bob wanted to be on hand if they did. So he chose to sleep in one of the jail's empty cells instead of the saloon.

It was not the first time Bob had slept in a cell, but it was the first time the door had been left open. It was also the first time he had been awakened by the smell of a cooked breakfast, brought to the jail by one of the saloon-girls. She couldn't have been much more than seventeen and was pretty enough to make Bob regret his decision not to spend the night in the saloon.

At first the morning was as quiet as the previous day. But then a battered old wagon arrived from out of town. Bob recognized its driver immediately. He was the young wrangler who had been in charge of the remuda of Sheriff Hicks's posse. Hal identified the lad as Tom Lorimer, the only son of a local homesteader and horse breeder. Tom was Hal's nephew.

Tom lived on his parents' homestead some distance from the town. Over the years they had withstood several Indian attacks. They had also turned their backs on farming by extending their homestead and turning it into a stud ranch, which they had registered as the Bar L. Hal said the family was much admired and respected by most people in Cottonwood. However, the fact that his sister had married Tom Lorimer's father might have clouded Hal's judgement a little.

When Tom had been the posse's wrangler, he had been unarmed. Today, he wore a huge six-gun. However, it seemed he had come to town for provisions, not trouble, for the old wagon pulled up outside the general store and the boy went inside. But he did not stay there for long. Looking more than a little flustered, the boy came out of the general store and headed for one of the saloons, while the storekeeper began to load the old wagon with supplies.

The boy had just entered the saloon when a gang of heavily armed gun-slingers rode into town, dismounted and went into the same saloon. But not before Hal had identified their leader as Daag Ward. Stocky, with long, dark hair and with a sallow, swarthy complexion, the renegade looked nothing like his much older half-brother.

'Bob, make your way to the back of the saloon,' said Hal urgently. 'Then look for a brown door. It leads to the rooms used by the girls when they are 'entertaining'. On your right you will see another door and that leads to the balcony above the saloon.'

Bob nodded in agreement. Although its barrel was shorter than a rifle, his new Winchester .44 carbine was still too bulky to be effective in confined spaces. So he picked up his old shotgun and hurried on his way. Hal followed shortly afterwards, but made his way to the saloon's front entrance.

Hal entered just in time to avert a tragedy. Although Daag Ward and his gang hoped to hire out for the Lazy Creek, the renegade had another reason for coming to Cottonwood. In a word, revenge.

The feud between Will Lorimer and Daag Ward went back years. To settle the feud once and for all, the renegade had devised a devious, two-stage plan, the first part of which was to provoke young Tom Lorimer into a gunfight. He and his gang had been hanging around Cottonwood hoping to catch the boy on his own.

Daag had little doubt he would be able to outdraw the youngster. After which, the renegade's twisted mind reasoned, the boy's death would cause his father to pick up his six-gun and come after him.

Although Will Lorimer had been more than useful with a six-gun, it was common knowledge that he had not carried one for several years. Even so, Daag had brought along his gang to ensure there could only be one possible outcome to any gun-play.

Unaware of the feud between the renegade and the Lorimers, Bob reached the brown door and went in. Climbing the steep and narrow stairs in boots one size to small for him was not so easy and he was breathing hard before he reached the top. His feet hurt. Yes, physically the boots were too small for him, but was he big enough to don the mantle of the Ranger who had originally worn them?

In front of him was a long corridor with a number of doors leading off it. Bob chose the first on the right and cautiously entered a large, dimly lit, thickly carpeted room. There were several plush sofas, each richly decorated in shades of gold and scarlet to match the carpet. The walls of the room were covered with large, erotic paintings of scantily dressed women.

'And to think I chose to spend last night in the jail instead of here,' groaned Bob. But nobody answered for the room was empty.

But there wasn't time to dwell on his mistake or study the paintings. Instead, he cocked both barrels of his shotgun, crossed the room, then cautiously opened the door to his right.

It was this door which led to the balcony. Surprisingly, it was poorly lit. Bob moved quietly to its banister and surveyed the scene below him. But not for long, for it was immediately clear that Hal, even with the help of the young Tom, was heavily outnumbered. A point not lost on Daag Ward who was gloating triumphantly over the situation.

'An old man with a badge and the Lorimer kid. It must be my lucky day. Whether you two draw or not, me and the boys are going to shoot. So make your play.'

'Sheriff Young already has,' shouted Bob, still on the balcony. As he did so, he thrust the shotgun forward to ensure that those below could clearly see both barrels.

It didn't take Daag Ward more than a moment to sum up the situation, but in that time Tom Lorimer drew his old Dragoon Colt. The youngster was lightning-fast. Yet he didn't fire. Perhaps it was because neither the renegade nor any of his gang reached for their six-guns.

But it wasn't the surprising speed of the youngster's draw that caused the outlaw gang to freeze. Only a madman would draw against a cocked shotgun in such a confined space. The risk of being ripped apart by buckshot was far too great. So without being ordered Daag Ward and his henchmen unbuckled their gunbelts and let them fall to the ground. Then, in almost perfect unison, they raised their arms and meekly walked to the jail.

There were at least a dozen gunmen

in the other two saloons waiting for the Lazy Creek's top hand, Brad Clark. However, when they found out Daag Ward and his gang had been captured by Bob, most of them rode out of town. None of them wanted to tangle with the Ranger who had not only captured Daag Ward but also, they believed, had outdrawn and killed Jack Crow.

Once all the gang had been safely locked up, Bob breathed a sigh of relief. He had passed his first test as a Ranger with flying colours. But the fancy boots of the real Bob McAllen still hurt his feet and, being one size too small, were difficult to remove.

Hal checked his Wanted posters, pausing briefly over one of them. There were rewards, totalling $1,000 for the capture of two of Daag Ward's gang, but Hal had nothing against the rest. So there was no legal reason to hold them in jail and they were released. Both men rode out of town so quickly that they left a cloud of dust behind them.

Bob had to get the three remaining

outlaws back to Fort Caddo; a job he could not do on his own. For most of the way back the trail wound its lonely way across the panhandle and there were several likely sites for an ambush. So even the help of Hal Young would not be enough if the two gunmen they had just released made an attempt to free Daag Ward.

So Hal decided to deputize his nephew, Tom Lorimer. The lad had already demonstrated his prowess with a six-gun and had been the wrangler for Sheriff Hicks's posse.

Tom readily accepted, thrilled to be working with his uncle and the Ranger he thought had outdrawn Jack Crow. However, the lad was barely seventeen, so his father's consent was required. As that was far from certain, Hal decided to accompany Bob and Tom to the Bar L and ask Will Lorimer himself. The trip would also give him a chance to visit his sister.

5

Hal arranged for a couple of reliable townsfolk to stand watch over the captured renegades. So with Tom driving the old wagon, the sheriff mounted on his fine roan stallion and Bob riding Rosa's little mustang, they left early next morning.

The little-used trail ran northwards. However, they were forced to proceed slowly as the storekeeper had heavily over-loaded Tom's old wagon, the wheels of which protested noisily.

After a couple of hours, the temperature began to rise sharply. It was going to be another hot day. As they rode on Bob could see, far to the west, the hills into which he had been pursued by Sheriff Hicks and his posse. Had he given the posse the slip he might have ridden on to Cottonwood to rest his horse and Hal would have probably asked the Rangers for help to capture him. So he might now be languishing in jail instead of Daag Ward. Such were the little ironies of life.

After another hour, they stopped to rest and water the horses. While Hal made temporary running repairs to the wagon, Bob used the time to get to know Tom a little better.

'You're pretty slick with that old Dragoon Colt. But it's a monster of a gun, with a kick like a mule; can you hit anything with it?' Bob asked.

Tom smiled ruefully, but did not reply. Instead, he drew the huge six-gun, cocked it and pulled the trigger in one smooth motion. But the old Dragoon didn't fire. It wasn't loaded.

'Pa won't let me use ammunition,' Tom explained. 'This old six-gun used to belong to my uncle. I've been practising drawing it almost every day since he got shot. I took it into town yesterday to see if the storekeeper would sell me the stuff I needed to roll my own ammunition. But he wouldn't because Uncle Hal had told him not to.'

'Tom, you got more guts than good sense to draw an unloaded gun,' said Bob.

During the rest of the slow trip, the wagon made noises that suggested it was about to break up. But it gave Hal the time to explain why acquiring the Bar L was of such importance to the Lazy Creek. Although it was only about 400 acres in size, all but five acres were lush, prime grazing land and those acres were covered by a lake. Even in the driest summers two streams flowed continuously down from the distant hills, then meandered lazily across the Bar L ranges into the lake. Although there were several waterholes, there was no other water in the vast area of the huge Lazy Creek ranch.

They arrived at the Bar L the following day and were warmly welcomed by Mrs Lorimer. She was much younger than her brother. Indeed, she looked no more than forty years old. Tall and elegant, but the roughness of her hands indicated she had done more than her share of the hard work needed to build up the Bar L from scratch.

Mary Lorimer's pleasure at the surprise visit of her elder brother was not diminished by his purpose for doing so. She had no objection to her son becoming a temporary deputy, only to him carrying a six-gun. Knowing how strongly his mother felt about it, Tom had wisely decided to remove the Dragoon just before they reached the ranch house.

Whilst her son saw to the horses and began to unload the old wagon, Mrs Lorimer led Bob and her brother into the ranch house, where her husband, Will, was waiting to greet them. He was older than his wife and as he struggled to get up, Bob could see that he limped badly.

'I keep telling him that he's too old to be breaking-in horses, but he won't listen,' complained Mary.

'Hush now, wife, our visitors don't want to hear about our problems,' rebuked Will gently.

'But Mary's right,' said Hal.

'Maybe, but I can't get a bronco-buster because the Lazy Creek hires those it can't scare off and I can't risk Tom getting injured, because he does most of the other work around the ranch,' said Will.

'It's about young Tom, I've come to see you,' said Hal.

Cottonwood's sheriff went on to explain what he wanted Tom to do. But the lad was almost indispensable and there were still many more horses to break in. So Will was doubtful he could spare his son, even if, by helping to bring the renegades to justice, Tom would be entitled to a share of the reward money.

Then Bob had an idea. The capture of Daag Ward had been achieved much sooner than had been anticipated. So he had a few days spare before he needed to start visiting the nearby homesteaders to gather news about the Lazy Creek.

'When I was not much more than a boy I lived with Indians who taught me how to break in mustangs,' Bob said carefully, not wishing to disclose anything which might link him to his former life as Jack Crow. 'So if you could see your way clear to letting Tom ride with us, I'd be happy to break in the rest of your horses.'

With the proviso that his son should only carry a shotgun, Will agreed. The relief on Mary Lorimer's face convinced Bob that his idea had been a good one. Yet he had no idea that staying to help would bring him in to contact with the other member of the Lorimer family and start another major change in his life.

Next morning, Bob and Hal breakfasted alone. Although it was barely dawn, Will and Tom had already eaten and had left to mend a broken fence. What time Mary Lorimer had risen to make their breakfasts, Bob dreaded to think. But then she never seemed to stop working. Even while he was eating his breakfast, she was outside, feeding the hens and collecting their eggs. While she did so, Hal filled in the Lorimers' background and the reason behind their refusal to let their son use a six-gun.

Ben King had been a bounty hunter and some time lawman when he met Will's sister, Annie, and married her. Although he was away most of the time, it was a good marriage and they had a daughter called Rebecca.

After a few years of marriage, Ben tired of life on the trail and bought a homestead almost next to that of Will. In between them was a small Mexican settlement, the owner of which had helped Ben to track down a gang called the Devil's Riders.

Most of the gang were hanged, but three escaped and, seeking revenge, attacked the Mexican settlement. Unfortunately, Annie was visiting the settlement at the time and she was killed by the outlaws. In fact, there was only one survivor, Carla, the daughter of the owner of the settlement.

Ben and Will went after the outlaws. They managed to kill two of them, but Ben died from the wounds he received and Will still limped badly from the bullet which struck his leg. The outlaw who escaped was little more than a boy: his name was Daag Ward.

Mary Lorimer then insisted that they should adopt Rebecca and they also took Carla under their protection. They then bought Ben's homestead and acquired the little Mexican settlement.

Every homestead granted free by the government was exactly 160 acres and the new owner was required to cultivate it for five years before he was granted full legal possession.

However, if he died or was killed, leaving nobody capable of farming the homestead, as in Ben's case, the land automatically reverted to the federal government. The cost of then obtaining that homestead was always one dollar and twenty-five cents per acre, regardless of which state it was situated in. That was far more than the Lorimers' savings but the bank in Cottonwood loaned Will the rest of the money providing his sister's brother, Hal, at that time a Ranger, became the sheriff.

After the shoot-out, Mary had made Will give up wearing his six-gun. But she had no idea that Tom had been secretly practising to draw one since he had got his Uncle Ben's Dragoon Colt.

But Tom had been seen to outdraw Daag Ward. Word of that incident would spread like wildfire and Bob knew from his own experience that it wouldn't be too long before some other gunfighter, looking to enhance his reputation, would challenge young Tom.

So when Will returned Bob took him to one side and, while Mrs Lorimer was out of earshot, told Will of his fears. To Bob's surprise Will not only agreed with him, but asked Bob to train the boy to shoot straight. To help, he even gave Bob a Navy Colt to give to Tom when his wife wasn't looking. But first Bob had to break in Will's horses.

Although the Lorimers ran a herd of about a hundred cattle, the little Bar L was far too small to be a real cattle ranch. Instead, the Lorimers raised quality horses for a living. They had a contract to supply the new US Cavalry.

The Bar L horses were worth considerably more than the Texas mustangs, thousands of which roamed freely all over the Texas panhandle. Before the War, thousands of mustangs were used by cowboys driving the big Texas herds up the old Shawnee trail to Sedalia or St Louis. Now that the War was over new trails would have to be opened up, then mustangs would be needed again.

Yet they were considered expendable and were generally sold at the end of the trail. Sadly, each mustang sold for a maximum of thirty dollars and sometimes much less. So breaking them in by specially hired bronco-busters was generally a swift and sometimes brutal experience. But that was not the way of an Indian, which was the way Bob had been taught.

As he did not want to be away from his prisoners any longer than was absolutely necessary, Hal returned to Cottonwood immediately after breakfast on the following day. Then, while the Lorimers watched, Bob selected the biggest horse still to be broken in and expertly roped him.

Next he led the big chestnut stallion into a small circular corral, especially designed for breaking-in horses. Then Bob released the rope and walked slowly to the centre of the corral. There he remained, absolutely motionless, staring hard at the big chestnut stallion.

To the amazement of the onlookers, the stallion moved close to the corral rails, then began to circle Bob, its tail twitching nervously. For some minutes Bob remained motionless as the stallion continued to circle, then he slowly moved away from the centre until he blocked the path of the stallion.

For a few seconds, both man and horse remained motionless, staring hard at each other. Then, suddenly, the stallion turned round and began to circle in the opposite direction away from Bob. Bob then turned around and waited for the stallion to complete its circle and come back to him.

Amazingly, the stallion stopped when it reached Bob, who continued to stare the beast down. Again the stallion turned and retraced its steps until, once more, it faced Bob, who had turned to meet it.

The process was repeated time after time. Never once did the stallion move away from the corral rails, nor did it ever try to pass Bob. One hour passed, then two. Then, long after the Lorimers had given up watching and gone about their daily chores, a change gradually began to take place.

Bit by bit, Bob moved slowly back to the centre of the corral. Yet still the stallion turned, but now as directed by the wave of Bob's hat. Domination of the stallion took most of the day to achieve, but a little before dusk, Bob decided the beast was just about ready.

Very slowly, he began to approach the stallion, making sure that this time he was always to one side of the horse, never head on. For the first time, he spoke to the horse, but his voice was scarcely more than a whisper. Then, he gently stroked the stallion's flank. At first, it shied away from Bob, yet it took no more than a few steps. Talking quietly to it all the time, Bob simply repeated the process until the stallion stopped shying away.

Then, as only a man trained in the ways of an Indian could do, he mounted the stallion. Bob had no saddle, reins or stirrups to help him. Nor did he wear any spurs. Amazingly, the stallion neither bucked nor bolted. Instead, it galloped steadily round the corral, only stopping when it was exhausted. Bob then dismounted and led the stallion out of the corral and into the stable. Talking to the horse the whole time, he watered and hand-fed the beast, before finally giving the animal a gentle rub down, the first it had received from a man.

Of course, the stallion was far from broken in. At dawn next morning Bob started again. And he started from scratch, as if the previous day had never happened. However, by noon, Bob judged the horse was ready to be ridden. This time he stayed on the horse for almost two hours before dismounting and leaving it alone.

After he had downed a large coffee and several of Mrs Lorimer's excellent cakes, he returned to the beast. But this time, before he mounted, he saddled it. The stallion bucked as he mounted, but it was a half-hearted effort and the horse soon adapted to being ridden.

After another hour, Bob dismounted and young Tom took over. The boy was a natural horseman and, without whip or spurs, soon gained control over the animal. Next, he rode the horse out into the panhandle and gave it a good long gallop while Bob started the process with the next horse.

This beast was far less co-operative and it took Bob a little over three days to break it in. The third was not much better but by the fourth horse Bob had regained the touch and feel he had had when he was a boy living with the Indians. So all the remaining horses were broken in within a few days.

However, by the time the last horse was broken in, Bob was almost exhausted, very stiff and extremely sore. It had been a long, long time since he had ridden without a saddle and he fervently hoped it would be even longer before he did so again. But a few days' rest and plenty of Mrs Lorimer's excellent cooking and he was as good as new.

While he was resting, Bob cleaned and checked Will's Navy Colt. The lightweight six-gun fired .38 calibre bullets which, in common with all handguns of the time, you had to make yourself. The process was widely called 'roll-your-own'. Much smaller, far lighter and with only a fraction of the kick or recoil of the massive Dragoon Colt, it was a far more suitable handgun for Tom Lorimer. However, Bob thought it was better for the youngster to discover that for himself.

So next day he took Tom out into the panhandle, well away from any disapproving ears at the ranch house, then began to test the youngster's ability with a six-gun. While he did so, the adopted member of the Lorimer family returned alone.

She had been visiting and helping to nurse a sick friend of Carla's. After the friend had recovered, Carla, instead of returning to the Bar L, had ridden down to the border to visit her relatives.

Will Lorimer had never been able to keep any secrets from his adopted daughter and told her everything that had occurred during her absence. She had a notoriously short temper and was furious that a stranger was teaching Tom, whom she regarded as her brother, to use a six-gun.

Without stopping to change out of her travel-stained clothes, she saddled her pinto mare and galloped off to find them, determined to stop her brother from becoming a deputy.

6

Tom Lorimer soon discovered there was much he had to learn about using six-guns. Yes, his draw was very fast, but he continually missed the stationary target Bob had rigged up. Bob let him continue shooting for a few minutes, then intervened.

'So what does your shooting tell you?' he asked.

'That I'm a terrible shot,' replied Tom disconsolately.

Bob drew and fired. He also missed. Then he measured out no more than ten paces and moved the target to that distance. He drew again and fired five shots. All hit the centre of the target.

'If your enemy is further than ten paces away, use a shotgun. If he is more than twenty paces away, use a carbine or rifle. You might live a bit longer if you remember that. Don't matter how fast your draw might be, if you don't hit your man, as sure as night follows day, he will get you,' concluded Bob grimly.

Tom tried again, but he still missed with most of his shots. The old Dragoon had been a fine weapon in its day, but it was big, heavy and had a kick like a mule. So Bob gave Tom the Navy Colt.

But before Tom could use it they were interrupted by a fast-approaching rider. It was Rebecca. The fiery redhead had found them by following the sounds of the firing. Still outraged, she dismounted. Crop in hand, she faced Bob.

'Why are you trying to get my brother killed?' she asked angrily.

Perhaps because of his own child-hood experiences, Bob had imagined Rebecca to have been little more than an infant when the Lorimers adopted her. Clearly he had been mistaken, for facing him was a very angry young woman about twenty years old. But neither her anger, nor her travel-stained clothes could disguise her rare natural beauty. Bob was stunned into silence by the sweep of her dark-red hair and her flashing green eyes. Fortunately, Tom came to his rescue.

'Becky! Bob is just trying to help,' he said, using her nickname which was exclusively reserved for close family and special friends.

'Help you to become the killer he is, you mean, don't you, Tom? You have killed lots of men, haven't you, Mr Ranger!'

Bob couldn't deny it.

'Anyway, Tom, Mama knows what you're up to and says you must come home at once!'

Without another word, she mounted her pinto and galloped furiously away. As the pinto went it kicked up a cloud of dust which covered Bob, yet left Tom untouched.

'Sorry about that,' said Tom as he tried to brush Bob down. 'I guess having her parents killed in a gunfight makes her a mite over-protective about her little step-brother.'

But Rebecca's words had stung Bob. He was really nothing but an outlaw masquerading as a Ranger. A faster gun or a noose would surely be his fate, unless he lit out for the border at the next opportunity. And yet, once given, he could not renege on the promise he had made to Jim Ward.

It was very quiet in the ranch house that evening. Mrs Lorimer was furious with her husband for giving Tom his Navy Colt and Rebecca treated Bob like a leper with cholera. So Bob decided tomorrow would be a good time to start visiting the neighbouring homesteads.

However, next morning, much to Bob's surprise, Rebecca offered to accompany him. He readily accepted; she was friends with most of the homesteaders and her presence might make them talk more freely. Or that was the reason he gave to Mrs Lorimer, even if it didn't ring quite true.

There was a slight delay because

Rebecca insisted on changing out of her working-clothes. While she did so, Tom saddled her pinto. She returned wearing a white lacy blouse. A golden bandanna replaced the plain neckerchief she used to protect her throat and a white Stetson kept her sometimes unruly red hair in place. Her riding-skirt was pure buckskin and her leather boots matched its colour perfectly. She rode using a man's saddle, yet Bob thought her the most attractive woman he had ever met.

Rebecca, for her part, wanted to know more about this Ranger who wanted to take her little brother away. For, much as she wanted to, she couldn't stay mad at Bob. There was a sadness in his eyes, only half-hidden by his smile, that reached out to her in a way she barely understood.

But Bob found her new mood very confusing. It was as if yesterday had never happened. Suddenly she began to tease him about the horse he was riding, Rosa's little mustang.

'Dear heavens! I've heard rumours about the Rangers being in difficulties, but is that poor beast the best you can do?'

'I lost my own horse in the hills between Tecos and Fort Caddo,' Bob replied.

'Wasn't that where the stage was ambushed by Indians and everybody on it scalped?'

'Yes, it must have happened just before I found them,' he replied.

'But you might have been scalped as well!'

'Only the good die young, so I was quite safe.'

'Bob, please don't joke about it.'

Her concern was clear. It was the first time she had used his first name and Bob felt ridiculously pleased. However, she didn't speak again until they reached the first homestead. Her presence helped to break the ice, but he learned nothing new about the activities of the Lazy Creek ranch. They fared little better at the other two homesteads they visited that day.

Mrs Lorimer's evening meal was superb. She seemed to have forgiven her husband and their relationship was back to normal. Rebecca seemed intent on making Bob feel more at home, then asked him about his life before he became a Ranger.

He told her the little he could remember about the murder of his parents and how he had been reared by reservation Indians. Of course, that was not quite accurate, but he didn't want to say anything which might link him to his past life.

However, at that point, Rebecca hurriedly left the room. Bob became concerned in case his story had reawakened bad memories about the deaths of her parents. But Mrs Lorimer told him not to worry.

Nevertheless, she went to look for Rebecca and found her in her bedroom, gazing at the stars, tears in her eyes. Adversity and their years together had forged a strong bond between them.

Rebecca unburdened her heart to the woman she regarded as her real mother.

'How terribly sad. When I lost my parents, at least I had you and Papa and a wonderful place to call home. Poor Bob had nothing.'

'You've changed your opinion a bit, haven't you, Becky dear?'

'A lot more than a bit, Mama. A whole lot more than a bit.'

Next day Becky again insisted on accompanying Bob. They drew another blank at the first homestead they visited. However, the owners of the next homestead to which they rode had quite a story to tell.

About three weeks ago, they had been visited by a dozen gunmen from the Lazy Creek, who told them that the big ranch intended to take over all the homesteads between it and the Rio Grande. As the Rio Grande was several days' ride away, this was a huge stretch of land.

The gunmen offered to pay a paltry sum for the homestead and said they would be back in a week with the money. If the homesteaders were not packed and ready to go by then, the gunmen threatened to burn down their farmhouse.

The homesteaders were packed and ready to leave within the allotted time. That had been two weeks ago, but so far the gunmen had not returned. The owners of the next two homesteads they visited told a similar tale.

On the way back to the Bar L they dismounted and stopped to rest their horses. Rebecca was in a pensive mood.

'I suppose you will soon be on your way to Cottonwood, taking my little brother with you,' she asked.

'Yes, Miss Lorimer. But you have my word, I will look after Tom.'

'But who will look after you, Bob?' she asked quietly.

'I'll get by, Miss Lorimer, I always have.'

'Bob, couldn't you be less formal?' Her voice was seductively soft.

'It would be a privilege to call you Rebecca.'

But that was not the response she was seeking and she stamped her foot on the ground in frustration. Bob, thinking he had somehow misunderstood her, began to apologize. Even as he did so, she interrupted him.

'Bob McAllen, you have turned me into a fast woman.'

But Bob had not the faintest idea how he had done so or why she was suddenly so angry with him. Desperately he tried again.

'Sorry to be so dense, but I don't understand you.'

Her reply took his breath away.

'I mean my family and closest friends call me Becky. But you will have to kiss me to earn that privilege,' she said quite shamelessly.

It was several seconds before he could respond. But this time his response met with her approval. Over dinner that night, she again encouraged him to call her Becky in front of everybody. Then, when the excellent meal was over, she surprised her family by curling up on Bob's lap and appearing as contented as a kitten which had fallen into a barrel of cream.

But it could be no more than a romantic interlude, for they had to say their goodbyes next morning. Again, Bob promised to safeguard Tom, but also had to promise Becky he would return as soon as he could.

At this, she threw her arms around him and kissed him passionately in full view of everybody. Then, somewhat embarrassed, but by no means displeased, Bob, accompanied by young Tom, reluctantly rode away.

As he did so, Mrs Lorimer sternly rebuked her adopted daughter.

'Becky, dear. No matter how much you like Bob, you mustn't be so forward.'

'But Mama, Bob has to have a sample of what's waiting for him when he comes back,' she replied cheekily.

'Get into the house at once, young lady. I don't know what's come over you,' scolded Mrs Lorimer. But, of course, she knew. The twinkle in her eyes betrayed her and told Becky her adopted mother was not as cross as she had tried to sound.

7

On the way to Cottonwood, each time they stopped to rest the horses, Tom tried his hand at 'rolling' his own ammunition and then using it to practise with the Navy Colt. But his father's gun continually misfired. He soon learnt that making your own ammunition was far from easy.

Bob had been doing it for years, but still put aside days when he did little else. The slightest lapse in concentration could easily result in a mistake leading to a misfire. Fast though he was with a six-gun, he had once been outdrawn. But a misfire meant it was the bounty hunter who was in Boot Hill and not Bob.

They stayed in Cottonwood only long enough to grab a hot meal and give their horses a short rest. Then, mindful of the promise he had made to

Becky to ensure Tom came to no harm, each prisoner was not only handcuffed but placed in leg-irons.

But these were not ordinary leg-irons for they had been adapted from a design which dated back to the Spanish Conquest. A heavy-duty leg-iron was locked into place round each ankle and the prisoners made to mount their steeds. Under the belly of the prisoner's horse, a heavy-duty chain was passed, each end of which was padlocked to the prisoner's leg-iron. So even if he escaped, the handcuffed prisoner could not dismount from his horse.

With Hal Young accompanying them, the party set off for Fort Caddo. On the way, whenever they paused, Tom practised with his newly acquired six-gun. But there was little sign of improvement and his efforts met with derision from Daag Ward. Otherwise, the journey passed without incident.

Their success was enthusiastically welcomed by Judge Bin. But as the outlaws had been captured alive, the reward money could only be paid out after they had been convicted. To expedite payment, the judge could have convened a trial and then handed out his usual summary justice. However, he wanted to demonstrate to a wider and more influential audience the merit of retaining Fort Caddo's Rangers. So the judge detailed two of its Rangers, both of whom had returned from their patrols earlier than expected, to take the outlaws to San Antonio to stand trial.

Such a show trial would obviously take a considerable amount of time to organize. So Hal and Tom returned home, both unaware that Judge Bin's decision, although perfectly sound, was to have tragic consequences and endanger the future of the Bar L.

Next day the two Rangers, together with Daag Ward and the other prisoners, left on the east-bound stage. Their departure was witnessed by a sizeable crowd, amongst whom were Daag's cronies, the gunslingers released by Hal.

Later that morning, Jim Ward returned from a lengthy patrol. Was it a coincidence that the Ranger captain's return had been delayed until after his half-brother had left for San Antonio?

Bob had little time to ponder the question as he was ordered to report on what he had found out about the activities of the Lazy Creek, which was well received. However, to his disappointment, neither Judge Bin nor Jim would be drawn into discussing what action, if any, they were going to take.

That night, when he was alone in Rosa's spare bedroom, Bob concluded that he had not yet done enough to be taken into their confidence. But he had other things, or rather, another person, on his mind. Namely, Becky. Her deep-red hair, flashing green eyes and bewitching smile gave him feelings he had never before experienced. Feelings he must suppress. Had she not already suffered enough from the violent death of both parents, and what other fate could there be for him? Even if he survived the dangers faced by every Ranger, sooner or later he would be exposed as the wanted outlaw he really was. A hangman's noose would be the result. He simply couldn't let Becky go through that.

Next morning, a young Mexican boy rode into Ford Caddo. Although barely fourteen and unarmed, he had been badly wounded. Nevertheless, he rode directly to the Ranger's office. Jim immediately sent for the doctor, while Bob did his best to stanch the flow of blood, a job he had been forced to do many times during the Civil War.

While they waited for the doctor to arrive, the boy told them his name was Manuel and that he was the grandson of General Jose Ferraire. Jim looked surprised and as soon as the messenger boy returned, sent for Judge Bin who arrived just a few seconds after the doctor.

However, neither the boy's name nor that of his grandfather meant anything to Bob, so while the doctor was attending to him, the judge explained that the Ferraire family were directly descended from Spanish nobility. Not only were they fabulously rich, their ranch, called the Alhambra, was so large that it incorporated the border town of Santa Madera. Moreover, although a Mexican living in Texas, General Ferraire wielded considerable political influence on both sides of the border.

Suddenly, the office door burst open and another Mexican lad burst in. He introduced himself as Juan, a wrangler who worked on the Alhambra. He explained that the Alhambra had been repeatedly attacked by a large gang of Americans. He and Manuel had set out for help but had been intercepted by the raiders and Manuel had been wounded. While he hid in thick cover, Juan led the gang away from him.

Fortunately, the bullet had passed clean through Manuel without hitting any vital organs. The doctor said that with rest and good nursing the young

Mexican should make a complete recovery.

News of the shooting of General Ferraire's grandson spread like wildfire through Fort Caddo, where, among the Mexicans at least, the shadow of General Ferraire loomed large. So large that Rosa offered to nurse Manuel. So he was carefully moved to her little cottage. But then her cousin, Emma, was the general's housekeeper.

Meanwhile, Bob was ordered to ride to the Alhambra with Juan, to establish who was behind the raids. He would be one Ranger against a small army. To supplement the shotgun already loaned to him by Jim Ward, he carried some special help: two brand-new Winchester .44 Carbines.

They set off next day. Almost immediately, Bob began to doubt Juan's story. The lad had changed into fresh new and expensive clothes. His boots were also new and clearly hand-stitched. His sombrero now sported a solid silver hatband with a strange design at the back of it. The boy's saddle must have cost at least $200. But the most amazing thing of all was the magnificent jet-black, unbranded stallion the boy rode. It simply towered over Rosa's pony, yet it was as nimble as the fleetest mustang.

The almost universal rate of pay for a wrangler was seventy-five cents a day. Not enough for a grown man to live on and certainly not enough to cover the cost of Juan's fancy gear. So, the only part of Juan's story that Bob could check didn't ring true.

Rosa's mustang had more trouble keeping up with Juan's magnificent stallion than did the pack-mule. So it was not until the sunset of the following day that they reached the Alhambra.

Bob was amazed by its incredible size. The massive, Mexican-style ranch house was enclosed by a formidable stockade and the area it enclosed was at least twice the size of the one in Fort Caddo.

The signs of recent conflict were everywhere. The sandy square of the courtyard was covered with patches of dried blood, made to look even more gory by the red rays of the dying sun.

Suddenly, the stately front door of the Alhambra swung open and a group of heavily armed *vaqueros* rushed out. They seemed delighted to see Juan and, amid scenes of much jubilation, escorted the lad and Bob into the Alhambra.

Bob found himself inside a massive hall. An impressive stairway led to a balcony. Polished granite blocks formed the floor and the walls were completely panelled in oak. Huge marble columns towered up to the ceiling, which was decorated in delicately painted murals depicting Biblical events.

At the foot of the staircase, ready to greet his visitors, was a distinguished-looking, grey-haired Mexican. The *vaqueros* approached him respectfully but Juan raced up and embraced him warmly, then ran up the magnificent staircase. The distinguished-looking Mexican turned and followed at a more sedate pace. Bob guessed he was General Ferraire, but who was Juan?

'Please follow me.'

Bob felt a slight tug at his arm. He had been so intent in watching Juan that he had failed to notice a well-dressed, Mexican woman of a similar age and appearance to Rosa, push her way through the crowd of celebrating *vaqueros*.

'Please follow me,' she repeated. 'During your stay with us, you will be occupying the American guest-room. I trust you will find it satisfactory.'

She led Bob down the hall and up another, slightly less grand, staircase. Then down a long passageway and through several doors. As she did so, she explained that she was the head housekeeper. She also told Bob her name was Emma and that Rosa was her cousin.

They came to an imposing oak door and went through it into the American room, which was really the lounge of a three-roomed suite. The walls of the room were covered with portraits of famous Americans, the one depicting George Washington being the most prominent.

'A bath has been prepared for you and dinner will be served in the great dining-hall at eight, but I shall be back before then,' said Emma as she left.

Bob went through the door leading to the bathroom. Sure enough, there was a bathtub full of scented hot water. He didn't need a second invitation. He stripped and plunged into the hot water. He was just beginning to relax when Emma walked into the bathroom armed with a razor and soap.

Just like her cousin, Rosa, she totally ignored Bob's protests and began to shave him. As he was still in the bath, there was little he could do to stop her without getting out and Emma had made sure that there were no towels within reach with which he could cover his modesty.

So, for the second time since he had become a Ranger, Bob found himself in a very embarrassing position while taking a bath. Emma was even more provocative than her cousin, flirting outrageously. After she had finished shaving him, she even suggested that Bob get out of the bath, but this was something he refused to do until she left. Emma was extremely amused by Bob's ever-increasing embarrassment, laughing uproariously as she left. And, like her cousin had once done, she took Bob's clothes with her.

Naked, Bob made his way through the lounge and into the bedroom. On top of the eiderdown, covering the largest four-poster bed he had ever seen, was an array of clothes of various sizes. Bob rummaged through them until he found some that fitted him and swiftly put them on, then struggled into his boots. He couldn't help looking at himself in the bedroom's full length mirror. Washed, shaved and in brand-new clothes, he looked a different man. Only the boots of a dead man reminded him of his past.

At five to eight, Emma returned. She

nodded approvingly, seemingly pleased at Bob's transformation. Then, she led him back downstairs and outside. Together, they walked across the courtyard to the great dining-hall, where she left him.

Situated at back of the actual ranch house and forming one side of the stockade wall, the great dining-hall had once been home to a garrison first of Spanish and then of Mexican troops. But it had long since been converted into something quite magnificent. Its walls were now panelled in exotic hardwoods and its floor had been made from mahogany, polished to a brilliant lustre.

At one end of the floor was a stage, upon which a small band was quietly playing some typically Mexican music. At the other end was a huge oak table capable of seating sixteen people.

Bob was led to his seat by a liveried servant, However, before he could sit down, the band stopped playing, then broke out into a trumpet fanfare.

General Ferraire, dressed in full military uniform, entered. With him was a young, aristocratic-looking Mexican woman. Her long black hair almost reached the shoulders of her pink evening gown. On her left hand, she wore a diamond engagement ring, the stone of which was huge and had a pinkish hue.

As the flunkey guided her to her chair, Bob could not help staring. Although he had never seen the woman before, something about her was oddly familiar. But far from being annoyed at his rudeness, she smiled.

'Come now, Bob,' she said softly, 'surely you know who I am? Much to my grandfather's consternation, we spent all of last night together.'

And they had. Somehow, Juan had been transformed into the dazzling beauty now standing before him.

8

Although there were only three for dinner, the meal was so lavish that it could easily have passed for a banquet. There were several courses; soup, freshwater fish from the Rio Grande, lemon sorbet, almost a whole side of beef, apple pie and water-melon. For a man who had been on the run just a few weeks ago, it was a feast beyond imagination.

During the meal, General Ferraire spoke little and only in Spanish, but Bob's former guide explained she was really Julia Ferraire. She had discovered that Manuel had planned to ride for help. So, unknown to her grandfather, she had disguised herself as a boy and gone with him. But, as she had previously told Bob, they had been seen leaving the Alhambra and been intercepted by the raiders. Manuel had been shot. Julia had led the raiders away from her cousin and then headed for Fort Caddo.

After the feast was over, Bob followed the general and Julia to an elaborately decorated but small lounge. In the centre of the lounge was a beautifully carved, circular table. As they sat round it drinks were served by yet another flunkey. As soon as he left, Julia locked the door and sat down again. The general began to speak. Much to Bob's surprise, his English was perfect.

'Julia says that you have come to protect us from these American raiders. But never have the Rangers sided with Mexicans against fellow Americans. But, if for once they have, what can one Ranger do against so many?'

Bob was well aware that the Rangers, although only 150 in number, had played a significant part in defending Texas during its short life as a republic. This had not only brought them into conflict with the Comanches but also with raiders from Mexico, who were trying to regain the ground they had lost during the Texas War of Independence.

Although it had been thirty years ago, that war had left a bitter legacy which Bob could do little about. But he could help the Alhambra against the raiders and told the general about the firepower of the two Winchester .44s he had brought with him. The general seemed interested but not fully convinced, so Bob changed the subject.

'Have you any idea who the raiders are and what they are after?' he asked the general.

'They are gunmen hired by the Lazy Creek. We just managed to fight them off last time, so now they are encamped near a water-hole about a day's ride away. My informants tell me they are waiting for some special re-inforcements, not expected to arrive for two more days.'

'The attack on the Alhambra would explain why Brigham Boyd had been recruiting more gunmen in Cotton-wood. But what has the Lazy Creek to gain by attacking you?' Bob was genuinely baffled.

'Water,' replied the general.

'But sir, it must be two or three days' hard ride to the Rio Grande . . . '

'More like four or five on that mustang of yours,' interrupted Julia drily.

'So I don't see where the Alhambra comes into it,' concluded Bob, ignoring Julia's remarks.

'To answer that,' replied the general, 'I shall have to give you a short history lesson.'

'Not the family history again,' groaned Julia.

This time it was the general who ignored her as he continued:

'My family was once one of the most powerful in Spain. My grandfather founded and ruled an empire which encompassed millions of acres south of the Rio Grande and, for a short time, almost as much in what is now Texas.

He also owned large orange-groves in California and a ranch as big as the Lazy Creek has now become.'

'But could one man run such a huge amount of land?' asked Bob.

'Yes, but only badly and my father was little better,' said the general. 'My grandfather supported Spain against the Mexican revolt and was executed for his pains. My father fought against Texas in what you call the Texas War of Independence. Then my uncle, who never agreed with anything my father did or said, took over the family estate and was killed fighting for the Confederacy against the Union.'

'Well at least we fought on the same side in that conflict,' said Bob ruefully.

'When I took over, I was only able to save the Alhambra and a few small settlements on the banks of the Rio Grande, the rest of our lands were lost.'

'But don't feel too sorry for us, Bob,' said Julia. 'When I marry my cousin, my future son, apart from inheriting the Alhambra, will also inherit twice as much land as we lost in California.'

'Julia,' rebuked her grandfather, 'it's quite improper for an unmarried woman to mention such things! And to dress as a man, ride like a man. It must stop. For the sake of your future husband, at least try to act like a lady.'

Yet the tone of his voice belied the harshness of his words. It was clear to Bob that he absolutely doted on his granddaughter and was immensely proud of her actions. What was still not clear to Bob was what the Lazy Creek had to gain by risking an all-out attack on the Alhambra.

They were interrupted by a polite tap on the door. Julia rose and unlocked it. Unbidden, several liveried flunkies and maids entered carrying trays laden with fruits, sweets and coffee. They fussed around for a few minutes until, at a signal from the general, they all withdrew. Julia relocked the door, then served the coffee.

While she did so, as if reading Bob's mind, the general began to answer

Bob's unspoken question.

'During the days of my grandfather, civil unrest was common, so he built up a large network of informants. As the Alhambra has passed down to succeeding generations of Ferraires, so many of the descendants of the original informants carry on the work their grandparents started.'

'Our own spy network,' interrupted Julia as she handed out the coffee. 'Unfortunately, it couldn't tell us that the Lazy Creek were planning to attack us!'

'Sadly true,' agreed the general, 'but at least we have an idea why. We have discovered that Brigham Boyd has set his sights on the post of Governor of Texas.'

'Governor!' exclaimed Bob in surprise.

'That's only to be the beginning.' continued the general. 'For some time our agents have been reporting that Boyd has been mixing with some very strange company. Renegades from both sides of the border have been rubbing shoulders with some of the ex-leaders of the Confederacy at the Lazy Creek ranch.'

'Do you have any idea what they are planning?' asked Bob.

'Not for certain, but we think it has something to do with the New Mexican Territories, possibly Boyd is raising funds for a new Confederate base to be set up there.'

'But that's ridiculous. Boyd's a Yankee,' protested Bob.

'A Yankee who lived in the South, working the steamboats,' replied the general. 'My information is that he was a second-rate gambler who barely scraped a living. He returned to the North when the War broke out, penniless. But he didn't fight. After the War was over, he bought the Lazy Creek. But where did he get the money from? Perhaps the Rangers know.'

'Sorry, but I don't think we have any information about his life before he came to Texas. However, we believe him to be behind the cattle-rustling that started as soon as he bought the Lazy

Creek. But we can't prove it,' admitted Bob ruefully.

'Well, my informants tell me that Boyd is the brains behind the gun-runners and within a very few days we will have conclusive proof. But what Texan jury would hang a gringo on the word of a Mexican?' concluded the general bitterly.

The discussion with the general had raised more questions than it answered and Bob had difficulty in sleeping that night for thinking about them. Next morning he was awakened by Emma. He had requested an early call, but had not expected it to be done by one of the senior members of the household. Yet Emma was as impudent and cheeky as ever, nothing like his image of a housekeeper and he had to shoo her out of the bedroom while he dressed.

Apart from about a dozen flunkies and serving-maids, Bob breakfasted alone. By the time he had finished, it was dawn. Bob went outside to see how well the Alhambra was being guarded. What he saw filled him with alarm.

The *vaqueros* who were supposedly keeping guard on the parapet of the stockade were busily chatting up the maids who had brought them their breakfasts. Except for those who were fast asleep.

The Tennessee Militia had specialized in what had become known as hit and run warfare and discipline was much less formal than in the regular army. Nevertheless, Bob had demanded that all the men who had served under him were professionals, always performing their duties to the best of their ability. The lives of their comrades had often depended on their doing so. The sloppiness displayed by the *vaqueros* in front of him endangered the lives of everybody in the Alhambra.

Bob resolved to confront the general immediately to resolve the problem. However, before he could do so, he was approached by another flunkey. In broken English, the flunkey requested

Bob to return to his rooms immediately.

When he arrived there, he found Emma waiting for him. With her was a brand-new set of clothes. In spite of all his protests, she insisted on assisting him to dress.

But not undressing him, which he did crouched behind the small mirror of the dressing-table. But he could not put on his new clothes without her help for they were a mixture of Spanish and Mexican and included an undergarment into which he had to be strapped. Emma found the whole episode hysterically funny, but this did not stop her from dressing him as rapidly as possible, then rushing him back outside to a waiting coach.

As with seemingly everything to do with the Ferraire family, this coach was far removed from the everyday stage-coaches which linked most towns in the West. This one was a glittering silver affair, covered in golden heraldic designs which Bob did not recognize.

Two blue-liveried coachmen sat on top, waiting to drive six handsome black stallions, all similar to the one ridden by Julia when disguised as Juan.

Julia, dressed in a formal, emerald-green costume, was waiting for him inside the coach. As they moved off, she explained they were on their way to attend mass in the cathedral at Santa Madera.

Bob had completely forgotten it was Sunday. In spite of the upbringing he had received in Tennessee, the day had little religious significance for him. However, the Ferraire family, as virtual feudal rulers of the Mexicans who lived in the area, were expected to attend mass twice each Sunday. As their guest, Bob was expected to accompany them at least once.

The town of Santa Madera was typical of many border towns. Hot, dusty and full of white adobe buildings, most of which were pretty run-down. The town had clearly enjoyed better days. But the cathedral, towering over the town square, was in pristine condition. Its stained-glass windows were superb. Bob was almost certain the statue of the Madonna, which dominated the square in front of the cathedral, was made of gold.

Inside things were even more elaborate. The floor was white marble. A huge silver cross stood on a golden plinth and the beauty of the murals on the ceiling had to be seen to be believed. Yet all outside spoke of poverty.

Julia led him up a flight of stairs covered in a red carpet, then into a box which was only ever occupied by the Ferraire family and their guests. The general was already there. As was the custom, he rose to greet his guest and Bob was embarrassed to receive a prolonged and standing ovation.

The mass, which lasted well over an hour, was conducted in Latin. Of course, Bob did not understand one word it. But he stood up and pretended to sing, or knelt as if in prayer, when prompted by Julia.

After the mass was over, the general stayed behind. On the way back to the Alhambra, Julia explained that the bishop, who had given the mass, was actually the younger brother of her grandfather and that the general stayed behind each Sunday to discuss the affairs of the cathedral and its congregation. It seemed that the younger Ferraire tended to the souls of the parish while the elder Ferraire ruled over their earthly lives.

So, it was not until later that afternoon that Bob was able to see the general and tell him what had to be done to improve its defences. But although he agreed to all Bob's demands, nothing could be done immediately, as everyone attended evening mass. However, Bob was excused from attending this time.

Work did not commence until dawn on Monday morning. But almost everybody pitched in and enthusiastically followed Bob's instructions. Perhaps their being translated into Spanish by someone as important as the general's granddaughter might have helped a little.

A few minutes before dawn on Wednesday morning, the time predicted by the general's spies for the Lazy Creek raiders to renew their attacks, all fortifications had been completed. Everybody was in their allotted place, fully armed and prepared to spring what Bob intended to be the final part of a trap. A trap unwittingly made possible by Daag Ward and his gang of gun-runners.

Bob took his place on the ramparts of the stockade armed with his new Winchester .44 carbine. By his side was the general. He had commandeered the other Winchester. However, in return, he had loaned Bob a powerful pair of field glasses.

As the first rays of sunlight pierced the gloom, Bob detected a large dust cloud which appeared to be moving slowly towards the Alhambra. In front of it rode a small army of riders.

Through the field glasses, Bob was able to identify a few of them as members of the posse which had pursued him.

But they were not the main cause of the dust cloud. As the riders crossed an isolated strip of grassland, from the dust behind them emerged two teams of horses. The first of these pulled a wagon full of men. The second team, made up of large carthorses, hauled a field gun. This formidable artillery piece and its gun crew were the reinforcements for which the Lazy Creek raiders had been waiting.

But its arrival had been predicted by the general's informants, so Bob was ready for it. He picked up the Winchester, ran down the wooden steps of the rampart, mounted Rosa's mustang, then galloped through the open gates of the stockade. He rode the mustang without a saddle, Indian style. It was the way he had been taught as a boy by the Crow Indians. After he left, the stockade gates were left open as part of his trap.

Bob reigned in the mustang. To the amazement of those watching from the stockade he clambered, clutching the Winchester, to the mustang's back, then stood upright. The extra height he gained extended the range of the Winchester and he fired all thirteen rounds into the dust created by the raiders as they traversed yet another strip of sandy ground. Although only a few of the bullets hit anything, the rapid rate of fire caused panic among the raiders.

Those in front wheeled away, desperate to get out of range, but their horses kicked up more dust as they did so. The swirling dust only added to the confusion, and because of it, the riders at the back could only hear the bullets. Unaware of the existence of the Winchester .44 and its capabilities, they wrongly assumed they were under attack from a large number of men. So they wheeled round, creating even more dust.

Through the billowing dust emerged the first wagon, its driver bellowing loudly at his team of horses as he turned them round. It was the last thing he did.

The new Winchester was, of course, breech-loading. Even standing precariously on the back of the mustang, it took Bob just a few seconds to reload it. His next shot hit the driver, causing him to drop his reins.

Panicked by the chaos, the wagon's horses bolted, but they were now facing the way from which they had come and their wagon crashed into the team pulling the field gun. Its driver had also been wounded and half-blinded by the swirling dust: he failed to take any avoiding action. Mayhem ensued and the sound of the collision could be heard in the stockade.

Satisfied that the first part of his trap had been successful, Bob slid down on to the back of the mustang and turned towards the open gates of the Alhambra. He could have galloped, but his own safety was not part of his plan.

As Bob had anticipated, once out of

range of his Winchester the raiders rapidly regrouped. Like a cavalry outfit, they charged back through the dust, narrowly missing the stricken wagons, musket-rifles primed and cocked.

As soon as they saw Bob they rode after him and opened fire. But a galloping horse does not make a good platform from which to shoot. All but one bullet missed and that hit the rump of Rosa's mustang. Gallantly, the little beast struggled on, but the raiders began to catch it up.

But it is not possible to reload a muzzle-loading musket-rifle or carbine from the back of a galloping horse. As one man, the raiders discarded their empty weapons and reached for their six-guns.

However, as young Tom Lorimer had discovered, the six-gun was only accurate at relatively close range. But the raiders were shooting from horseback some distance behind a moving target. Most of them emptied their six-guns, vainly trying to hit Bob. And that was exactly what Bob had hoped they would do. He was in more danger of being struck by lightning than one of the raider's bullets. He rode into the stockade, unharmed.

The raiders, eyes fixed on Bob, swept through the open stockade gates into the trap set by Bob. Had the raiders looked up, they could not have failed to see that the rampart walls were lined with heavily armed *vaqueros*.

Each *vaquero* had two Musketoon rifles. These were Confederate copies of the British Enfield .54-pattern musket-rifle. Ironically, they had been purchased from Daag Ward and his gun-runners by one of the general's agents posing as a rebel leader from Mexico.

Using Bob's other Winchester, the general opened fire. This was the signal for the *vaqueros* to do the same. At point-blank range a murderous hail of bullets poured down on the raiders from the ramparts. Most of the raiders had no answer as they had emptied their six-guns. In a matter of seconds half of them were killed or seriously wounded.

But there was no respite for the survivors. The general reloaded and kept firing his Winchester. When it was empty, only six raiders were left alive. Six-guns already emptied, they surrendered before the *vaqueros* could use their second Musketoons.

Then, dressed in her guise as Juan, Julia swept past Bob on her great black stallion. Following her were about a dozen riders. Bob recognized some of them; they were the house-flunkies. They charged towards the stricken wagons.

However, this was not part of Bob's plans, but as his own mount had been wounded, there was nothing he could do. Nevertheless he was desperately worried about the safety of the general's granddaughter. From the look of alarm on his face, he also had not been aware of Julia's intention to ride out of the stockade.

But they need not have worried.

119

Apart from the wounded wagon driver, the only men left at the scene of the crash were the gun-crew of the field gun. Mostly unarmed, they surrendered without a fight.

From start to finish, the battle had lasted less than ten minutes. Of the raiders who had attacked the Alhambra only the gun-crew, one of the wagon drivers and six actual raiders survived. The only casualty on the Alhambra's side was Rosa's pony and that would survive, even if it might not be fit to ride for several weeks.

Bob was instantly acclaimed a hero. However, he thought he had done little to deserve such praise. Success had been mainly due to the two revolutionary Winchester .44s and perhaps the experience he had gained whilst serving in the Tennessee Militia under General Natham B. Forrest.

9

The ramparts were fortified. The cannon was raised on to the fortifications in such a way that its range of fire protected the approach to the stockade's gates. Then, rough justice at the end of a noose was the fate of the surviving Lazy Creek raiders. Except for one. After witnessing the hangings and a practice-firing of the cannon, he was allowed to leave unharmed. Free to tell anyone who cared to listen how the Alhambra dealt with those who attacked it. The general hoped his brutal actions would deter any other would-be raiders.

Once the freed Lazy Creek raider had left, the Ferraire family gave thanks in church. Again, as their guest, Bob was also obliged to attend. But the general let it be known that it was to be a private occasion. As a result, the streets of Santa Madera were deserted as the general's glittering coach was driven through them.

Then, it was fiesta time and the celebrations started. Bob had experienced nothing like it. He was the guest of honour at the fabulous banquet held in the state room. Outside, the *vaqueros* and the citizens of Santa Madera partied, ate, drank and danced the night away.

Next day, Bob informed General Ferraire he must soon return to Fort Caddo. He also requested the loan of a horse until Rosa's pony had recovered from its wound. However, the general insisted that Bob stay for one more night.

Bob was presented with yet another set of clothes, every bit as well-made and elaborate as the white ones he had worn at the cathedral. But these were black. However, the sombrero had a solid silver hatband. On it was a design similar to the one Julia had worn when she had been disguised as Juan. But this silver band had a modification at the back which transformed it from an expensive ornament into something which, in Bob's hands, was to prove to be a deadly weapon.

Bob was informed by Emma that the solid silver hatband was one of a set which had belonged to the Ferraire family for several generations. To refuse it would be considered an insult. As Bob had no wish to offend, he accepted.

If the earlier banquet had been formal, this one was doubly so. Unlike the first, all festivities were conducted entirely in Spanish. So, as soon as it was polite to do so, Bob slipped away and joined the *vaqueros*' party outside. But not for long, for although he was made to feel most welcome, Bob could not keep up with their drinking, so begged to be allowed to retire to his bedroom.

But it was not until two more rounds of tequilas had been ceremoniously downed that Bob was allowed to leave. His departure had been deliberately delayed by the *vaqueros* to give someone the time to get to his bedroom suite and prepare a surprise.

That someone was Emma and her naked body was the surprise. She was wild, willing and passionate but she was not Becky. Even so, they made love all night. Then, next morning, they shared a hot tub and an intimate breakfast in the quiet of a near perfect dawn.

After they said their farewells, Bob made his way outside, only to find more surprises waiting for him. The *vaqueros* had formed two lines to make a guard of honour. Their friendly nods and winks as he walked between the two lines indicated that they had all been conspirators in arranging his night of passion with Emma.

At the far end of the line stood General Ferraire, shotgun in hand. It seemed he was also aware of the events of the previous night. But he was not in the least angry, for he had suggested it to Emma, who had been more than willing to oblige.

General Ferraire formally presented

Bob with the shotgun. It had been made in England and was of superb quality. But the surprises were not yet over. Julia led her magnificent black stallion towards him.

'Grandfather informs me that when the society ladies of California ride, they ride side-saddle on pretty little ponies and my future husband will expect me to do the same. You need a good horse and I cannot think of anybody else to whom I would rather entrust him.'

'He's magnificent,' said Bob. 'I thought I knew something about horses, but I've never seen anything like him.'

'That's because his sire was a pure blood from Andalusia, a province in Spain which has always been noted for breeding horses of rare quality.'

At a signal from General Ferraire a *vaquero* carrying a magnificent new Mexican-style saddle approached and stopped in front of Bob.

'A good horse needs a good saddle,'

said the general. 'I can never repay the debt I owe you for saving the Alhambra. So this is just a token of my appreciation.'

An hour later Bob rode away from the Alhambra on the black Andalusian stallion, which he had decided to call Andy. He wore the first set of clothes Emma had given him. She had carefully packed the other new outfits into his saddle-bags. He left the pack-mule with Rosa's pony, which was on the way to a full recovery. His new steed loped untiringly along the trail and the return journey to the Fort Caddo was soon completed.

However, led by a young lieutenant aptly called Freshman, the US Cavalry had arrived during Bob's absence. Freshman's lack of experience did not prevent him throwing his weight around. His first action had been to commandeer the Rangers' office. His next, to institute a state of martial law, which effectively put him in charge of maintaining law and order. Something he lost no time in telling Judge Bin.

Bob had barely dismounted when he was approached by a trooper who instructed Bob to report to the lieutenant at the double. Bob declined.

'First, I have to get my horse rubbed down, then I have to report back to my boss. A Ranger captain outranks a cavalry lieutenant, I think.'

Looking worried, the trooper doubled back to Lieutenant Freshman who was outraged by Bob's reply. He immediately summoned both the judge and Jim Ward to what was now the lieutenant's office to lecture them on the matter.

Having ensured his horse was being properly looked after, Bob then slowly walked to the Rangers' office, which was now occupied by Lieutenant Freshman.

'McAllen, when I give an order, I expect it to be obeyed instantly,' snapped the lieutenant.

'As long as that order is to your troopers, and you remember I am not one of them, you have every right,' Bob replied calmly. 'I answer to the Rangers.'

'McAllen, when you speak to me, you are to address me as sir. As for the Rangers, they have been officially disbanded. I am the law now. My first duty will be to track down the Indians who ambushed the stagecoach you found. Then I am going to make this wasteland safe for decent white folk to live in. Something the Rangers have failed to do. But until the Indians have been dealt with, neither you nor any civilian will leave Fort Caddo.'

It was on the tip of Bob's tongue to tell the lieutenant that the ambush had not been carried out by Indians, when he thought better of it. If the cavalry rode into the panhandle chasing non-existent Indians they would be out of everybody's way.

'As you wish, Lieutenant. By all means go after the Indians. But I suggest you get Jim to show you how it is done. He's been fighting Indians all his life and he's still alive.'

'McAllen. It will be a long and dark day before I take your advice. Now to the manner in which you address me. I do not want to have to mention it again.'

'Good,' replied Bob, 'because the last time a lieutenant addressed me he called me sir. But you may call me Mr McAllen.'

Before Lieutenant Freshman could reply, Bob walked out of the office. He had better things to do than argue with the lieutenant. Chuckling to themselves, the judge and Jim Ward followed him. They went into the saloon and gathered round the judge's old table. Bob told them about the events at the Alhambra and of Brigham Boyd's supposed political ambitions.

Although the last of the Rangers had been officially disbanded, the devious judge had managed to get himself reappointed as the circuit judge. Apart from continuing to dish out his brand of instant justice, he intended to use his new position to organize a lobby to get the Rangers reinstated.

'It won't happen overnight,' said the judge. 'The Yankee carpetbaggers are everywhere at the moment, but their power won't last. The future prosperity of Texas is out there, grazing on the panhandle. So the real power will swing to the big ranch owners. It doesn't matter where they originally came from, or which side they fought for during the Civil War, they will want a law agency that understands and looks after their interests.'

'Which was why Stephen Austin formed the Rangers in the first place,' said Jim.

The judge looked thoughtful for a while and drank another cognac before speaking.

'Of course, there's no need for us to spread the news that the Rangers have been disbanded. If anyone asks you directly, you must tell them the truth. But otherwise, just act as if nothing has happened. We might just get away with it for long enough to put a stop to Brigham Boyd. In the meantime, perhaps it's time to call in a few favours.'

The judge would not be drawn further on the subject but he did have some more news. Daag Ward had escaped, killing Reb Morris in the process. It was believed the renegade had reformed his old gang and was working for the Lazy Creek but in Mexico. Bob confirmed that General Ferraire's man had purchased the Musketoons that they had used against the Lazy Creek's men from Boyd's own gun-runners, but he didn't know if their leader had been Daag Ward.

But Brigham Boyd still needed water. Although there might not be enough water on the Bar L to satisfy all the Lazy Creek needs, neither the lake nor the two streams feeding it had ever dried up. As far as Boyd knew they were only protected by the lame old man and his son.

But nothing could be done that

night, which Bob spent on Rosa's sofa, as Manuel still occupied the spare bedroom. Nor could anything be done next day, as Lieutenant Freshman's troopers continued to guard all the exit routes out of Fort Caddo.

Bob fumed at the delay, but at least it gave him time to devise a plan. As soon as possible Jim Ward was to ride to Cottonwood and enlist Sheriff Hal Young's aid. After all, he was Mrs Lorimer's brother. Bob would ride directly to the Bar L and remain there until Jim and Hal arrived with a wagon.

Only then could the Lorimer women-folk be evacuated to Cottonwood, as their wagon was too far gone to be used again. Once in the little town they could stay with Hal's family until it was safe to return. Bob and Jim would remain at the Bar L to help protect it.

It was a simple plan, but even so it required the wiles of Judge Bin to get Lieutenant Freshman and his troops out of town, long enough for Bob and Jim to slip away unnoticed.

In the meantime Bob risked further embarrassment by taking another bath at Rosa's. But it was necessary. For although he hated to admit it, his brand-new Mexican saddle had given him sores in places that no cowboy would ever mention. So he spent a large part of next day rubbing linseed oil into the saddle to soften the part upon which he sat.

10

How Judge Bin accomplished it was a mystery to Bob, but two days later, flags flying and bugles blowing, the US Cavalry rode out of Fort Caddo on a patrol. Amongst much pomp and circumstance, they rode west towards the New Mexico border, leaving only a relatively inexperienced non-commissioned officer and one trooper behind to enforce Lieutenant Freshman's orders. They were easily diverted from their duties. Both were young and inexperienced so no match for the wiles of the women of the saloon which the judge often frequented.

While they 'entertained' the young troopers, Bob and Jim slipped quietly out of Fort Caddo, then split up. Jim rode south down the main trail, then cut across the panhandle to Cottonwood. Bob rode eastward through the hills and then on towards the Bar L.

While the two troopers were recovering from their 'entertainment', Judge Bin also slipped quietly out of Fort Caddo in a covered wagon. In the back of it was Manuel Ferraire with Rosa to nurse him.

Bob had chosen to wear the first and most workmanlike set of new clothes presented to him by the Ferraire household. But he wore the black hat with its special silver band. As well as the shotgun and his old Army Colt, he still carried the two Winchesters. His saddle-bags contained the rest of his clothes and extra ammunition, leaving little room for food. So by the time he reached the Bar L, he was looking forward to again sampling Mrs Lorimer's cooking.

As Bob approached the Bar L, he saw two horses tethered outside. There was no reason for alarm, yet a feeling of unease spread over him. He had developed a sixth sense for survival. It was something which he had first felt during his Indian upbringing, then he had experienced this strange, eerie feeling during the Civil War and again later whenever he had ridden into danger on the outlaw trail.

Without knowing why, he instinctively knew something was not right. He slowed the big stallion down to a walk and approached the Bar L warily. Everything looked the same, therefore it took him longer than it should have done to realize what was wrong. But he eventually did. So instead of approaching the ranch house normally, he yelled a greeting as if this was his first visit.

'Hello, the house. Would appreciate getting some water for my horse.'

There was no response, so he repeated the call. After a few more seconds Mrs Lorimer appeared at the door. She gave no sign of recognition as she replied.

'Use the trough yonder for your horse. If you'd care for some coffee, you're welcome.' Her eyes desperately flashed warning signs for him to leave, but Bob ignored them.

'Mighty good of you, ma'am. I'll see to my horse, then I'll take up your kind offer.'

With a look of despair that lived with Bob for many days, Mrs Lorimer went back into the house. Bob took his time watering Andy, then stopped behind the big stallion and made an adjustment to his special silver hatband. Then, casually, he made his way to the ranch house.

Inside, Will Lorimer lay semi-conscious on the floor, blood oozing from a head wound. Young Tom was gagged and handcuffed. Becky, bound and gagged, sat on a kitchen chair, the front of her gingham dress ripped open to the waist. Standing over her, gun drawn, was Sheriff Hicks. On the other side of the room was Walt, one of the deputies who had helped to take the body of the real Bob McAllen to Fort Caddo. Walt's six-gun remained pointed at Mrs Lorimer, a mistake which was to prove fatal.

'Well, well, look who we have here. If

it's not the mysterious Ranger,' said Sheriff Hicks. He looked at Bob. 'A fine new horse and a brand-new outfit. My, you've done pretty well for yourself. You can keep them, but I'll have your silver hatband. Use your left hand to get it and move it carefully.'

Bob, silently raging at what had happened to Becky, spoke not a word. Cautiously, his left hand moved as if to remove the band. But the back of the band seemed to catch on something. Slowly, Bob moved his left hand further behind his head. Then, faster than any of the onlookers could follow, a small silver object flashed through the air and buried itself in Sheriff Hicks's throat. The sheriff gasped once, then slid to the floor, quite dead.

Simultaneously, Bob drew his Colt with his right gun hand. Walt had followed the silver knife instead of watching Bob and his six-gun was still pointing towards Mrs Lorimer. Desperately, he turned it towards Bob, but as he did so, he was struck with the force of a sledge-hammer and flung against the wall. But he felt no pain, he was already dead.

Torn between her injured husband and the distraught Becky, Mrs Lorimer hesitated. But Will was as tough as they come and although still groggy insisted on Becky being looked after first.

Bob holstered his Army Colt, retrieved his knife, wiped the blood off the blade, then cut Becky's bonds. Mrs Lorimer removed her gag. Shocked and embarrassed by the half-naked state of her body, Becky fled to her bedroom, followed by Mrs Lorimer.

'All right, old man?' asked Bob anxiously as he helped Will Lorimer to his feet.

'Sure. Guess you've earned the right to call me Will, but less of the old man. I'll be fine, see to my boy.'

Bob again approached the body of Sheriff Hicks. He bent down and fumbled through the dead man's pockets until he found a set of keys. The third one he tried unlocked Tom's handcuffs. Coughing and spluttering, Tom removed his gag.

'I've never seen anything like that. Where did you learn that trick with the knife?'

'Talk about it later,' said Bob firmly. 'If you're up to it, let's get these bodies out of here before the ladies get back.'

'This is still my house so I'll help Tom,' growled Will Lorimer. Then he smiled as he continued: 'I think Becky has more need of you than these vermin.'

Bob agreed and hurried to Becky's bedroom, then knocked gently on the door. Mrs Lorimer opened it and beckoned for him to enter. Becky had already changed out of her tattered dress and was now wearing a simple white blouse and black skirt.

'I think I'll burn this,' said Mrs Lorimer as she picked up the remains of Becky's dress and made for the door. Bob looked at her in alarm, thinking he should not be left alone with Becky in her bedroom. But Mrs Lorimer smiled and closed the door behind her. As she left, Becky sensed Bob's unease.

'Don't worry. I'm a fallen woman now with no reputation left to worry about.'

He could have been sympathetic, but he wasn't. There had been occasions during the Civil War when his junior officers had gone into shock after a particularly bloody battle. Experience had taught him that a firm but understanding response was usually the best approach.

'Becky. You're not the first woman to suffer like this and you won't be the last. Please don't let me hear you talk badly about yourself again.'

Tears trickled down her face. Bob's resolve melted and he sat down beside her.

'Come on,' he said gently. 'Let it all out. Whatever else I am, I'm your friend.' A few minutes later, Mrs Lorimer returned to find a tearful Becky cradled in Bob's arms.

'Becky, it's all over,' she said kindly.

'Bob, can we girls have a few minutes alone?'

He left quietly and went to help the Lorimer men dispose of the bodies. Will and Tom had managed to drag them out of the ranch house, but were having difficulty in lifting the dead weight of their bodies into the old wagon. However, with Bob's help, the gruesome task was swiftly completed.

The ancient wagon was then driven into the panhandle and the bodies dumped into the ravine. But not before Bob had retrieved their Army Colts and spare ammunition. They were going to need all the six-guns they could get their hands on.

When they returned, Will had to rest. The old wagon was about finished. Its juddering ride had caused his leg to ache badly. Tom went to look after the dead men's horses which had been hidden behind the barn. In doing so, he found that each horse carried a Springfield rifle.

Meanwhile, Bob busied himself with

Andy, unsaddling and rubbing down the big stallion. Then Tom helped to take Bob's saddle-bags, the two Winchesters, the old Springfields and his new shotgun to his bedroom.

While Bob washed, shaved and changed into his black clothes, the inviting smell of the evening meal wafted into his bedroom, reminding him he had hardly eaten since leaving Fort Caddo. So he hurried to the kitchen.

Looking almost recovered, Becky served the meal. The meal was just reheated stew and beans, but Mrs Lorimer had a way with food that made the ordinary taste special. Bob enjoyed every mouthful and happily accepted seconds. However, during the meal, he could not fail to notice that Becky, wide-eyed with surprise, kept staring at him. Mrs Lorimer noticed and decided to explain.

'Bob, you've changed so much, we hardly recognize you.'

'You mean I've got some decent

clothes,' he replied.

Mrs Lorimer smiled. She thought far more than Bob's appearance had changed, but she kept those thoughts to herself.

Sensing the need to raise everybody's spirits, Bob told them about the Alhambra, cutting short the details of the attack and concentrating on the embarrassing position he found himself in when Emma shaved him in the bath. Even Becky found that amusing. Over coffee, Will asked him something that had been bothering him.

'Tell me, Bob. When you rode up, how did you know something was wrong?'

'Will Lorimer,' scolded his wife, 'don't you think Becky has suffered enough today?'

'No, Mama, it's all right. It might help to talk about it. Besides, I'd like to know.'

Bob looked at Becky admiringly. If it was possible for her to go further up in his estimation, she now did. So he answered the question by rubbing his stomach.

'It felt wrong. I couldn't figure it at first, then I realized something was missing.'

'What was that?' asked Mrs Lorimer, now as interested and puzzled as her husband.

'Why, the smell of your excellent food,' Bob replied. 'Something had to be wrong if you were not cooking.'

Bob's reply brought forth much merriment

'Where did you learn to use a knife like that?' Tom asked for the second time.

'As a white boy raised by Indians, I had to be at least as good as the rest. But don't ever try that trick. It took hours of practice, every day, for many years.' Bob looked hard at Becky as he continued. 'But I'm not proud of it, I've killed many times.'

'How many?' asked Tom before his mother could stop him.

'Too many. But Tom, no matter how

145

good you think I am, there's bound to come a day when I will meet some young kid faster with a six-gun than me.'

Becky's sharp intake of breath was audible to everyone in the room. But Bob continued: 'Sometimes, when I can't sleep, I like to think that I didn't have a lot of choice in becoming a 'killer' as Becky once called me, but Tom, you do.'

'But with the Lazy Creek on the rampage, what choice do I have?' protested Tom.

'There's a big difference between defending your home or loved ones, and hiring out your gun to the highest bidder. Anyway, promise you won't reach for your gun unless you have no other choice. Then, never draw without firing. The only reason I'm sitting here now is because when Hicks had the drop on me, he talked instead of shooting.'

Mrs Lorimer had been right, Bob had changed, even if, as yet, he had not realized it.

11

Next morning, Will predicted that a real Texas storm was brewing. Yet, although there was a strong breeze, it was still fine. Bob handed his spare Winchester to Will and they rode out into the panhandle. Will needed to get used to firing the high-velocity cartridges. However, in spite of the ever strengthening breeze, the senior Lorimer proved to be a capable shot. In fact, he adjusted to the new Winchester far more easily than Bob had.

While he practised, Will explained how Sheriff Hicks and his deputies had managed to seize the ranch. Apparently, the raid had not been premeditated. Acting for their real boss, Brigham Boyd, the sheriff and his two deputies had come to the ranch to trade for water rights.

Mrs Lorimer had invited them inside

for coffee. But finding Will unarmed, they had overpowered him and taken control of the ranch. Hicks hoped that an appreciative Brigham Boyd would give him some of the money he would have had to spend for obtaining the water rights.

But the sheriff still had Tom Lorimer to deal with. Under severe duress, Will had told the sheriff that his son was out on the range mending fences. However, Hicks had been instructed by Boyd not to harm the boy. His fate was to be settled by the Lazy Creek's latest recruit, Daag Ward, even though the renegade was mainly operating south of the border.

So the sheriff tied up Becky and waited for Tom to return. When he did, the lawman allowed Tom to dismount. Then, without warning, he ripped open the front of Becky's dress. Taken completely by surprise, Becky screamed involuntarily. Tom rushed in to find out what had happened and found himself staring down the barrels of three six-guns. There was nothing the youngster could do but surrender.

After the sheriff had handcuffed Tom, he sent his other deputy to the Lazy Creek for reinforcements. He felt they might be needed in case Mrs Lorimer's brother caused trouble. After all, Hal was a lawman.

The deputy had only just left when Bob arrived. At first, Sheriff Hicks didn't want Bob to find out what had happened in the ranch house, so he gagged Becky and Tom to prevent them shouting a warning. But when he saw the solid silver band on Bob's hat, the sheriff's greed got the better of him.

However, Hicks had left his rifle on his horse. He was not about to tangle with the man who he thought was either Jack Crow or the man who had outdrawn the outlaw. So he decided to lure Bob into the ranch house. But the crooked lawman was unaware that Bob knew the Lorimer family. So he saw nothing strange when Bob called out to the ranch house. As a result, he sent Mrs Lorimer to meet Bob and instructed her to invite him into the house.

As Will finished his tale, the wind suddenly began to blow much harder, making accurate shooting impossible. By the time they had returned to the ranch house, dark thunderclouds raced across the sky. By the time Bob had unsaddled Andy and settled the big stallion safely in the barn, the sky had turned inky blue. Then it began to rain very heavily.

Bob raced to the shelter of the ranch house as lightning flashed and thunder rumbled threateningly. Hastily, doors were bolted and windows shuttered. Then the storm struck. But inside, all was snug and dry. Bob remembered when, as a boy, he had been caught out on the prairies in similar storms. He guessed correctly that the Lazy Creek reinforcements would seek shelter.

Over a bowl of Mrs Lorimer's superb beef-and-vegetable stew, Bob outlined his plans to evacuate Mrs Lorimer and

Becky. But the women would have none of it.

'This is my home and as long as my husband stays, I stay,' said Mrs Lorimer.

'It's my home too,' said Becky quietly. 'The Rangers sent Bob, so when he doesn't return, they will know there is trouble and send help. Surely we could hold out until then?'

In spite of Judge Bin's instructions to say nothing about the disbanding of the Rangers unless directly asked, Bob felt the Lorimer family had a right to know the truth. But it made no difference, they were all determined to stay.

Becky seemed the most surprised and perturbed by Bob's news. While the others discussed how best to defend the ranch, Bob noticed that she remained unusually quiet. Thinking her silence was due to her ordeal yesterday, he tried to bring her into the conversation, but his efforts met with little success.

Yet later in the evening, when she went to the kitchen to help Mrs

Lorimer prepare supper, she engaged her mother in earnest conversation. The upshot of which was that Mrs Lorimer persuaded her husband and Tom to go to bed early, thus leaving Becky alone with Bob. As soon as she was certain the rest of the family had settled down for the night, Becky spoke accusingly to Bob.

'I have two questions for you, Mr Ex-Ranger. Firstly, why haven't you asked if Hicks did anything else to me yesterday, and secondly, if the Rangers didn't send you, why did you come back?'

'The answer to your second question is simple, I made you a promise that I would return. As to your first question, I didn't ask to avoid causing you any more distress.'

'But don't you want to know, or don't you care?' Becky said angrily.

'Whatever happened was forced on you, so it makes no difference,' replied Bob gently.

'It does to me,' said Becky bitterly

and abruptly left the room.

Next morning, although the thunder and lightning had gone, the wind was still gale force and it was still raining heavily. Over breakfast, Becky seemed a little more like her old self and began to tease Bob about his fine new clothes and his magnificent black stallion.

'When you were here last, you looked like a saddle tramp. Now look at you! Did you rob a bank?'

'Not quite. The horse, saddle, shotgun and clothes were all presents from the Ferraire family. Perhaps I shouldn't have accepted them, but they were most insistent.'

Becky seemed satisfied with his reply. But now that it had been decided that they were all to stay and fight, she demanded to be more than just a spectator when the Lazy Creek attacked, forcing Bob to review their position. There was enough food and water to withstand a siege and the rainstorm meant that the outside timber of the ranch house would be too wet to catch fire. So the Lazy Creek would have to rush the ranch house to take it.

Apart from Bob's shotgun and two Winchesters, Will had two old muzzle-loading rifle-muskets. Both were Colts, the Special Model 1841, a wartime variation of the Springfield. Bob gave them to Tom and instructed him on how best to defend the back door.

Over the years, circumstances had forced Mrs Lorimer to become as proficient as any infantryman at reloading the Special Models, so she became Tom's loader. Bob also gave her the six-gun taken from Sheriff Hicks's deputy. Bob and Will were to defend the front.

As well as Bob's spare Winchester, Will had Tom's old Dragoon six-gun. Bob gave Becky Hicks's Colt and showed her how to load his shotgun. To do so, meant she had to stay by his side and that meant he could look after her. Bob also had a Winchester and his own Army Colt. Then there were the two Springfield rifles taken from Hicks and his deputy. Bob loaded them and put them by the front door.

There was nothing left to do but wait. The rain eventually ceased and the wind blew the clouds away. Suddenly it was hotter than ever and the ground began to dry.

Mrs Lorimer and Becky excelled themselves in preparing the evening meal. Lashings of roast beef with all the trimmings were followed by hot apple pie and cream with plenty left over to eat cold next evening. Providing they lived long enough to enjoy it, thought Bob grimly.

He took first watch and blew out the lamp to enable him to see outside. Moonlight lit up the surrounding panhandle. But nothing stirred. Where were the Lazy Creek gunmen? Bob guessed they would arrive sometime tomorrow well before Jim Ward and Hal could reach the Bar L. Asking them to bring a wagon in which to evacuate Mrs Lorimer and Becky had not been one of his better ideas.

As if by magic, as his thoughts dwelt on Becky, she suddenly appeared and sat down beside him. She had changed into her best dress. White, its elegant simplicity perfectly complemented her natural beauty, or so Bob thought. Yet he said nothing.

'I'm sorry I was so unreasonable earlier on,' she said softly and gently slid her arm round Bob's waist.

A cold shiver ran down Bob's spine.

'Forget it, Becky. It's me who should be apologizing. I guess no man can really understand the ordeal you went through.'

His arm suddenly developed a mind of its own and, in spite of Bob's avowed intentions, slid round her shoulders, pulling her closer to his side. To his surprise, instead of resisting, Becky snuggled into him as if it was the one place in the world she wanted to be. And it was.

'Tell me about your first pa,' he said gently.

'I never really knew him. When I was

very little he was always away. Then one day, after he had been away for months, he suddenly returned and told us he had got a place to homestead and enough money to keep us going until the first crops were sold. So we moved in. At first it was good, but then the little Mexican settlement next to us got attacked by outlaws when my real ma was visiting it. They killed her and my pa got shot killing them. The Lorimers bought the homestead and the settlement and adopted me.'

'It must have been a terrible time for you,' said Bob. 'I wouldn't want you to go through anything like that again.'

'Now it's my turn not to understand,' said Becky.

'Becky, during the War, I was an officer in the Tennessee Militia and I didn't receive a pardon.'

'That's why you joined the Rangers,' Becky said softly.

'Partly. But what I'm trying to say is that one day my past could catch up on me. I can't let you take that risk.'

Becky tensed and sat bolt upright.

'How dare you.' Her whisper had more venom in it than a canyon full of rattlesnakes. 'Do you think us Texas girls are made of such poor stuff that we quit because there's a chance that something bad might happen?'

'No, but — '

'But me no buts, Mr Ranger. In case you've forgotten, there's a load of Lazy Creek men heading our way. When they get here, I'll be right by your side. If I have to, I'll fight and shoot to kill, because they threaten my home. And I'll do the same, if and when anybody else threatens us!'

Becky took a deep breath. Too late. Her hot temper had betrayed her feelings.

Us. The word hit Bob with the force of a sledge-hammer. The world seemed to stand still. Not so Becky. From growling tigress to purring kitten. Her transformation was instantaneous and she was back in his arms before he could move.

'You will just have to get used to my moods,' she said as she kissed him. 'But I said us and I mean us.'

This time Bob kissed her. Keeping lookout was interrupted as she returned the favour and they were still arm-in-arm when Mrs Lorimer appeared. She smiled at the couple.

She had made fresh coffee and intended to stay with her husband through his watch. Reflecting on her life with Will, it had been hard and sometimes dangerous. But there was little she would have changed. She just hoped Becky would be as lucky.

12

Unaware of the fate of Sheriff Hicks the dozen Lazy Creek reinforcements had seen little point in riding through the storm. So they had taken shelter in a line shack. It was a tight squeeze as it had only been built for four, but at least it had been dry. Nevertheless, they were on their way as soon as the storm blew itself out.

Tom was on duty when the reinforcements eventually reached the Bar L. But they pulled up well short of the ranch house. Just as Bob had done a few days earlier, Brad Clark sensed something was wrong.

'Sheriff Hicks, show yourself,' he yelled.

Bob cursed himself. He should have tethered the horses of Sheriff Hicks and his deputy outside the ranch house.

'Sheriff Hicks isn't here,' replied Will

Lorimer, taking charge of the situation.

But not for long. One of the raiders fired at the ranch house, but the bullet fell short. Will's didn't. Again the superiority of the Winchester's fire power was proved as one of the raiders crashed to the ground, quite dead. Unaware that the ranch house was defended by two repeating rifles, Clark ordered his men to charge. It was the last order the Lazy Creek's top hand gave. Will and Bob poured lead into the charging riders and Clark was one of the three of them who were dead before they too, hit the ground.

The rest of the raiders wheeled their horses round and galloped away only stopping when they were well out of range. There was a brief discussion, then a rider rode rapidly away, Bob guessed he was going to get even more reinforcements.

The next few hours passed without further incident. The raiders camped well beyond the range of the Winchesters and, in spite of the heat, lit a fire to cook their food. The fire spluttered a little at first, but it hadn't taken the sun of a hot Texas summer long to dry out the land. The storm was almost forgotten.

With Becky at his side, Bob took his turn to keep watch. Bob scanned the raider's camp with the field glasses given to him by General Ferraire. But he could only see five Lazy Creek men by the fire. Frantically he scanned the whole area until he located the other two gunmen creeping through a large, waist-high clump of tumbleweeds, near to the camp. Bob watched them until they suddenly dropped out of sight. Becky told him they had dropped down into a gully which ran past the back of the corral and continued right round the back of the ranch house.

Bob grabbed the Springfield, gave it to Becky, then reluctantly left her to watch the raiders' camp. He raced to the kitchen window and waited for the two raiders to attack. But they didn't. Instead, they remained just out of sight, effectively ensuring that nobody could leave the ranch house to go for help.

Just after midnight, when Tom was guarding the back of the ranch house, a small pebble struck the kitchen window, followed by several more. Tom called for Bob to come and help but before he arrived, a voice called softly to the ranch house.

'Don't shoot, we're coming in.'

Silently as a ghost, out of the shadows, emerged Jim Ward. Tom hastily unbolted the kitchen door. The big captain of the Rangers quietly entered, Bowie knife in hand. There was blood on its blade.

Following closely behind him was Hal Young. Cottonwood's sheriff carried two ammunition belts and two Navy Colts, both of which had fancy carved butts. Hal dropped his booty on the kitchen table.

'Don't worry about the two Lazy Creek men at the back of the ranch house,' said Jim, as he wiped the blade of his Bowie knife. 'In town, they may be something. But in the open, fancy guns ain't no match for an old Indian fighter like me.'

'Each of them had one of these,' said Hal throwing two fifty-dollar pieces on the table. 'I guess that's the going rate to run us off the Bar L.'

The night vigil was kept by Will Lorimer aided by a continuous supply of coffee from his tireless wife. But two hours before dawn Hal slipped out of the now unobserved back door and disappeared into the night. Silently but slowly he circled the ranch house before making his way to the back to his wagon. It had been left a little over a mile away after the sharp ears of the Ranger captain had heard gunfire coming from the direction of the ranch house.

The wagon was still in the grassy gully where it had been left, its horses still grazing contentedly. As the first signs of dawn began to lighten the sky, Hal scurried round collecting branches from a nearby clump of cottonwoods.

He attached them loosely to the rear of the wagon in such a way that their leaves swept across the ground as the wagon moved along.

Hal cracked his whip and the horses broke into a gallop until he found a large sandy patch of ground just out of sight of the encamped raiders. Then, as dawn broke at last, Hal again forced the horses to gallop, this time in circles, the trailing branches kicking up a dust cloud as they did so.

An hour after Hal left the ranch house, Bob and Jim did the same, then made their way along the gully towards the camp of the raiders. They moved as silently as any Apache, so it wasn't surprising that the lone guard did not detect them in the tumbleweeds near the camp, where they waited until dawn.

As daylight spread over the panhandle, the guard's attention was distracted away from the ranch house towards the dust cloud which seemed to be coming from just over the horizon. He rapidly awoke the sleeping gunmen. Muttering and cursing at being disturbed so early in the morning, they arose to look at the dust cloud, presenting their backs to Bob and Jim, still hidden in the tumbleweeds.

But the advantage was lost as Jim, six-gun drawn, stood up and ordered the gunmen to throw down their weapons. They did not. Each gunman spun round to face Jim, drawing their six-guns as they did so.

Jim fired, hitting two of them, but Bob, taken completely by surprise by Jim's sudden move, could only get off one shot from his prone position. Three gunmen died instantly but the bullets of the other two struck Jim full in the chest.

Desperately, Bob rolled to his right, and began a move he had used many times in the Tennessee Militia. Two bullets thudded into the spot where he had been crouching. He continued rolling to his right. Each time he came to the top of his next roll, he fired. The speed of his movement caused the two gunmen to miss. Bob didn't, and both gunmen were fatally wounded.

Breathing heavily, Bob picked himself up and as soon as he was sure that all the gunmen were dead, made his way over to where Jim lay. One glance at his blood-soaked chest told Bob that it was all but over for the gallant captain of the Rangers.

'Always knew it would end like this, some day.' Jim barely had the strength to spit out the blood in his mouth and continue. 'But I just couldn't shoot them in the back like my half-brother would have done. I'm a Ranger and that's not our way.'

They were the last words spoken by the bravest and most honourable man Bob had ever met and they stayed with him for the rest of his life. In that instant, Bob became that which at first he had only sought to impersonate by wearing a pair of *dead man's boots*, a Texas Ranger.

Nevertheless, his military training made him search the gunmen. Each of the five dead gunman had a fifty-dollar piece which Bob collected. But he found nothing to prove that the money had been paid to them by Brigham Boyd.

So he took his hat off and waved it in the air. His solid silver hatband reflected the rays of the sun as he did so. It was the prearranged signal that this part of the battle had been won. But it had been a victory dearly bought. With one last glance at the body of his fallen friend, Bob turned and walked back to the ranch house.

13

The mood was sombre. Jim Ward's death hit hard. Although few of those who attended his impromptu funeral could claim a long or close acquaintance, the captain of the Rangers had earned their respect and admiration.

But the battle was far from over. Bob secretly feared that the worst was still to come. While they were waiting for the rest of the Lazy Creek's gunmen to arrive, the men found something to do.

Young Tom and Hal unloaded stores and ammunition for the Winchesters from his wagon; Will Lorimer exercised the horses in the main coral. Then all three men got into the wagon and collected the bodies of all the gunmen and dumped them into the same ravine that had been used to dispose of the bodies of Sheriff Hicks and Deputy Walt. But not before they had collected all the weapons and ammunition from the dead gunmen, giving them even more firepower for the forthcoming battle.

While the other men were busy, Bob was rolling bullets for his Army Colt. However, he was interrupted by Mrs Lorimer. She had made up a picnic basket and suggested that Bob take Becky for a short ride to take her mind off the killings. As there was no sign of the Lazy Creek gunmen, Bob readily agreed. In any case, his big stallion needed the exercise.

Later that afternoon they rode to the lake. Becky led Bob to the spot where the two streams flowed into the lake. Waist-high alfalfa grass grew in abundance and small birds warbled in the reeds near the water's edge. Yet a few minutes' ride away, the harsh brown scrub of the panhandle stretched in every direction, as far as the eye could see.

It was not hard to see why Boyd was so determined to take over the Bar L.

But a man with great political ambitions, Boyd could not be seen to be involved in the fighting. So he sent almost all of his remaining gunmen, together with Daag Ward and his gang of gun-runners to crush the Bar L, while he remained at the Lazy Creek ranch. Both decisions were to cost him dearly.

The picnic was a delightful success. Mrs Lorimer had surpassed herself and there was an abundance of cold chicken and beef, homebaked rye bread, cheese and apple pie. All washed down by the sweet and pure stream-water. And then there was Becky: what more could a man want, thought Bob.

But it was only a dream; even if he came through the next few days in one piece, the Rangers were finished. He had to tell Becky about his past. When she found out he had been deceiving her all the time, her fiery temper would ensure the end of their relationship. In that case, he would move on to Mexico or try his luck in the wilds of New

Mexico. But he could at least enjoy this one afternoon with her.

All too soon it was getting dusk. Reluctantly they packed up and returned to the ranch house. Becky sensed that something was troubling Bob, but she wrongly assumed it was the forthcoming attack, so did not question him about it.

The time which had flashed by when he was on the picnic, seemed now to stand still while he waited for the Lazy Creek raiders to reach the Bar L. But arrive they did and there were enough of them to virtually encircle the ranch house. Under the leadership of Daag Ward they stayed well out of range. This time it was to be a siege rather than a full-blooded attack.

However, patience and plenty of food are required to complete a successful siege and the renegade and his men had little of either. Their cause was not helped by the aroma of Mrs Lorimer's marvellous cooking while they ate nothing but hard tack. So, on the fifth night of the siege the renegade leader decided to attack. But the delay was to have disastrous consequences to more than just himself.

The strength of the Bar L ranch house almost proved to be its undoing. For while its side walls were impenetrable, one of them had no windows. Once the raiders reached it, they could reach the roof in comparative safety. Then, while those inside the ranch house were pinned down by heavy fire from the rest of his men, the gunmen on the roof could force an entry through the roof.

But it was a full moon that night and Bob had guessed the renegades' plan, so was ready for the attack. At first the raiders, illuminated by moonlight, took heavy casualties from the crossfire of the Winchesters, strategically positioned by Bob. But then his luck ran out and clouds covered the moon. Shooting became guesswork. Several raiders reached the roof, where they remained until dawn.

Dawn was greeted by a continuous

barrage of fire from the raiders as they tried to pin down those inside the ranch house, while the gunmen on the roof tried to break in. Bob knew that only by going outside could they be prevented from doing so. But fully exposed, nobody could survive the murderous hail of bullets directed at the ranch house. Nevertheless, going outside was what Bob intended to do. He might just live long enough to get at least some of the gunmen on the roof.

He explained his plan to the others. Tears in her eyes, Becky begged him not to, but Bob's mind was made up. His plan was interrupted by an even heavier and more rapid barrage of shots, but they were not aimed at the ranch house. Nor was the return fire from the singleshot musket-rifles of the raiders. For a few minutes, the outside was a battlefield, then all went quiet.

But only for a moment. A barrage of bullets hurtled towards the roof of the ranch house and bodies began to fall from it. Again all went quiet. Those inside looked at each other in amazement. What was happening? A familiar voice answered their unspoken question.

'Hello, you in the house. It's all over, you're quite safe to come out.'

It was Judge Bin. But he was the least of the surprises waiting for Bob as he cautiously stepped outside. With him was General Ferraire and about twenty mounted cavalry, half of whom were dressed in the uniform of the Mexican Army. The rest, most surprising of all, were made up by the US Cavalry, led by Lieutenant Freshman. Several of the assembled carried Winchester .44 carbines.

But explanations had to wait. Only a handful of gunmen lived through the combined cavalry assault. They were made to identify the dead and help bury them. But Daag Ward and two of his henchmen were not among them; once again the renegade had somehow managed to escape.

Judge Bin noted all the names of the

dead men. However, he ignored the hundred dollars each of the outlaws possessed. Nor were the troops permitted to touch the money. So it was left to Bob, now officially classed as a civilian with the disbanding of the Rangers, to collect the money. Together with the money already collected from the bodies of the first Lazy Creek raiders, it amounted to almost $4,000. In the aftermath of the Civil War, a not inconsiderable fortune.

General Ferraire assigned half a dozen of his men to help Mrs Lorimer clear up the mess and damage caused by the raiders. Then, outside, on a hastily constructed range, she and Becky cooked a meal for all the troops. It took virtually all the Bar L provisions to do so, but was well worth it. Seldom, if ever, had troops eaten so well.

Over the meal, explanations for the day's extraordinary turn of events were sought and given. It seemed the judge had triggered the whole thing off when persuading Lieutenant Freshman to go searching for non-existent Indians. But they had run into a Quahadi raiding party and chased them down to the Rio Grande.

Freshman was unaware that the Quahadi, a sub-tribe of the Comanche, were fearless, white-hating warriors who ran from no one. This raiding party simply led the young lieutenant and his men into a trap, set by their formidable warchief, Quanah Parker. In spite of having a white mother, Quanah Parker was bitterly opposed to the white man settling on what had previously been Indian-occupied land.

Heavily outnumbered, the lieutenant knew his troops would take heavy casualities if they stayed to fight. Yet all but one avenue of escape had been cut off by the Quahadi. That was across the Rio Grande and into Mexico. However, that was forbidden by the treaty between America and Mexico. So to do so would certainly cost the lieutenant his army career.

But the lieutenant put his men before

his career and crossed into Mexico. Still chased by the most ferocious Indian tribe of all, they ran into a Mexican border patrol, which had being trying to catch Daag Ward and his gang of gun-runners. Fortunately the Mexicans were of sufficient numbers to deter the Quahadi.

But the damage had been done. In return for his men being allowed to recross the Rio Grande, the lieutenant surrendered himself to the senior Mexican officer. Yet instead of being taken prisoner, he found himself and his troops being escorted to the Alhambra.

Judge Bin was already there, having returned the general's grandson, Manuel. A council of war was called and information shared. It was decided that the two military forces would combine under the leadership of General Ferraire and go after the gun-runners. Such a move would have undoubtedly caused an international incident if found out, but it was hoped that Judge Bin's presence would legitimize any action taken. To give the last rites to any of the Mexicans fatally wounded during the expedition, the general's younger brother, the bishop of Santa Madera, accompanied them.

Not expecting to be followed on American soil, the gun-runners made no effort to cover their tracks. Following them led General Ferraire's force directly to the normally heavily guarded Lazy Creek. But Brigham Boyd had sent Ward's gun-runners and most of his gunmen to capture the Bar L. Had Daag Ward not delayed his attack on the ranch house, he and his men might have accomplished their mission and returned in time to defend the Lazy Creek.

The general was not one to miss an opportunity. He attacked. Within a matter of minutes the few gunmen left at the Lazy Creek had been overrun. A few minutes later a cache of arms, including a dozen new Winchester carbines, and details of sales to Mexican rebels and Indians were discovered. Brigham Boyd's fate was sealed.

Gun-running to Indians was a hanging offence. Judge Bin knew all about Boyd's powerful political connections and decided to hold the trial before he could use them. In less than an hour the Lazy Creek boss was found guilty. While the troops built a temporary gallows, Boyd, a Catholic, called for a priest to make his last confession.

Boyd's involvement with the Confederate conspirators and the gun-running had been a ploy. Once he had become governor, he intended to betray both parties and claim credit for their capture. In doing so, he hoped to achieve enough fame and popularity to be able to run for the presidency. The rustling was to provide funds so to do.

Boyd also confessed to masterminding the stagecoach ambush. The woman on the stagecoach had been his first and only legal wife. His son had been the result of an earlier affair with a woman who, sometime afterwards, had come into a considerable inheritance.

When the War broke out, Boyd, then a Mississippi riverboat gambler, left the South and his real wife. He returned to New York where he went through a bogus marriage with the mother of his son, as she was now a wealthy woman. She died in mysterious circumstances just before the end of the War.

After the War, Boyd purchased the Lazy Creek, but his real wife had tracked him down and threatened to expose him as a bigamist. So Boyd had arranged for Daag Ward and his men to ambush the stage she was on, then kill every one on it.

It had been Boyd's idea to scalp the victims, making it look like an Indian raid. He didn't know that Indians didn't normally scalp women nor did he know that there was a Ranger on the stage. When his men found out that they had killed a Ranger they panicked and bolted. Daag rapidly followed them. He had been so busy with the scalping that he failed to examine the dead Ranger.

Had he done so, Bob realized, the renegade would have been able to expose him as an impostor. It seemed that fortune had been on his side since the day of the ambush. But how much longer could his luck hold out?

Boyd had been duly hanged. The general had then burnt down the Lazy Creek ranch house, saving only the Winchesters and their ammunition. These he distributed among the troops. Then they had ridden non-stop to the Bar L arriving just in time to save it from falling into the hands of Daag Ward.

Explanations over, troops fed, their horses rested, the general and his men left the Bar L. It was essential the Mexicans returned to their side of the border before they were missed.

Judge Bin left at the same time, but his destination was Fort Caddo. There were claims to be made. Among the dead were several wanted men, with rewards for their capture, alive or dead. The judge guessed the total value of their reward money would exceed $2,000, all of which the Lorimers and Bob were entitled to collect. It seemed there was no end to his good fortune.

14

The men were exhausted after everything that had happened and little work was done on the Bar L next day. They relaxed and discussed the fairest means of sharing out the cash taken from the raiders and the reward money they were due. Bob argued that the Lorimers should take the lion's share and he and Hal split the rest. But Will flatly refused, insisting that it should be Bob who had the biggest share. Eventually, Bob reluctantly agreed to taking half, which amounted to $3,000.

Meanwhile, Mrs Lorimer and Becky, between cooking the meals, planned how to spend at least some of the cash. A new wagon, provisions to replace those used up by the troops, more general supplies, new pots and pans and other household goods went on the practical list. Lots of material to make new dresses, more to make new curtains, new hats, gloves, tobacco for the men and a special present for Bob were a few of the things which went on the other list.

At first light next morning, the women, accompanied by Tom, set out for Cottonwood. They planned to do a lot of shopping, stay overnight then return next day in their new wagon, which young Tom was to choose.

Hal drove them in his wagon. Bob reckoned that for the moment it was safe for Tom to go. But not for long. After all the fuss died down, Daag Ward would come gunning for Tom. The renegade had to do so because Tom had been seen to outdraw him in Cotton-wood. He had to kill the boy in a gunfight to restore his reputation as a top gunslinger. And he knew that, although young Tom was as fast as they come, he couldn't hit a barn unless he was inside it.

Both Hal Young and Will Lorimer were too old to go up against the renegade. But that wouldn't stop them from trying to protect Tom and getting themselves killed in the process.

No, Bob decided it was up to him to complete the job he had started when he first captured Daag. He put his share of the cash taken from the raiders into a small sack and left it and a note explaining what he intended to do in Becky's bedroom. Then he told Will what he planned. In spite of Will's objections, Bob saddled Andy and rode off.

Bob had spent almost two years on the owlhoot trail and could still think like an outlaw. Daag had to find somewhere to hole up. Santa Madera and Fort Caddo were far too risky and he was too well known in Cottonwood to go there. That left Tecos, back where it had all started for Bob. And there was a major problem: to find the renegade Bob needed the help of the one man who could identify him as Jack Crow.

It was a strange feeling to be back in Bart's saloon. It was almost as empty as the fateful day of the shoot-out. So much had happened to him since then, it seemed like a lifetime ago. Perhaps it was, he certainly felt differently, but what would Bart do?

There was a star on Bart's chest, but he was still running the bar. It seemed he had just had a visit from a whiskey peddler, for he was busily stacking bottles of rye behind the bar. He smiled and stopped working.

'You'll be Bob McAllen, the Ranger the whole county is talking about,' he said loudly enough for those in the saloon to hear him.

Still smiling, he served Bob. As Bob went to pay him, Bart shook his head.

'Your money is no good in here. I ain't about to forget how you helped my old friend Jim Ward when you was last here. Bad news travels fast, and I'm sorry to hear what happened to him. He was a good man, nothing like his no-account step-brother.'

'It's Daag I'm looking for. Have you seen him lately?'

'Sure have,' replied Bart. 'He's been hanging around here since yesterday. Been bragging how he's fixing to call you and the young Lorimer kid out.'

'Know where I can find him?' asked Bob.

'Yep, but I ain't telling. He's got two bushwhackers with him. They will backshoot before you can get near Daag. Your only chance is to take him on in here, while I watch your back. I'll see he gets to know you're looking for him, if you want.'

Bob nodded in agreement and Bart spoke to a barfly. The man was just drunk enough to go to Daag's shack and just sober enough to remember the message. While he was doing so, Bob got his shotgun and put it on the counter.

'You might need this,' he said to Bart.

Bob didn't have long to wait. Daag, full of confidence, swaggered into the saloon. But he was alone. He smiled sardonically as Bob turned towards him and then sauntered towards the bar as if he hadn't a care in the world. And he hadn't.

Too late Bob realized the significance of the renegade's smile. His two bushwhacking friends had somehow got into the back of the saloon and were standing behind him. But if Bart could get to the shotgun on the bar, Bob thought he might have a chance.

'Bartender, step right away from that shotgun or one of my friends will plug you,' said Daag, as if reading Bob's mind.

Bart sidled away from the shotgun, knocking over Bob's beer glass as he did so. He bent down as if to get a mop. For a brief second, the two gunmen behind Bob were distracted and Bob went for his six-gun.

He had not the slightest hope of surviving the unequal shoot-out, but he might get Ward before his bushwhacking friends got him. But he wasn't going to make it easy for them. As he drew, he flung himself to the right, as he had done many times before. Still in mid-air, he fired. Ward's gun had barely cleared his holster when Bob's bullet hit him, low in the stomach. The impact caused him to double up. Then with a deep sigh, the renegade fell forwards on to the floor.

As Bob crashed to the ground, bullets from the bushwhackers flew over him. Before Bob could reply, the saloon was shaken by a mighty blast and filled with smoke which enveloped Bob. Then came screaming and a strange gurgling noise. But no more shots came from the bushwhackers.

As the smoke cleared, Bob saw why. Standing at the far end of the bar was Bart, holding the strangest-looking weapon Bob had ever seen. It looked like a single-barrelled shotgun, but the end of its barrel had been flared out to wider than a man's fist. It was a very old blunderbuss which Bart kept under the bar. He had picked it up when pretending to get the mop. Bob's shotgun had acted as a perfect decoy.

Old as the blunderbuss might have been, it was still deadly. As Bob looked across the room he saw that the two bushwhackers had been torn to shreds by the buckshot it fired. It was over and he was still alive.

'I'm obliged,' said Bob, smiling at Bart.

'Don't be. I forgot to lock the back door after the whiskey-drummer left,' said Bart ruefully.

Bob left next morning, knowing he was almost a wealthy man. The reward money for Daag Ward had risen to $1,500 and his two henchmen were worth another $500 each. Of course, he would share it with Bart and young Tom. It wasn't his fault that Daag had escaped after the lad had helped catch him in Cottonwood. Yet that still left Bob with a whole lot of reward money, which, added to the rest, brought his personal fortune to almost $4,000. But without Becky, that meant nothing.

The men were unloading the new supply wagon when Bob reached the

Bar L. His wave told them it was all over at last. Becky rushed out of the ranch house to greet him, scolding him and laughing at the same time. But he held her at arm's length as he told her who he really was and explained how he had changed clothes with the real Bob McAllen.

Without a word, she turned away and walked towards the ranch house. Bob's heart sank, his worst fears seemed to be realized. But she returned a moment later with a parcel in her hand. It was the present she had bought in Cottonwood.

'Sit down and take off your boots,' she ordered.

Bob did as he was told. As always, it was a struggle, for the boots of the real Bob McAllen were always going to be a size too small.

She gave him the parcel. Inside it were the most exquisite pair of boots he had ever seen. They fitted perfectly. Becky smiled at him.

'Right from the start, I guessed who

you were and Uncle Hal confirmed it. He had your Wanted poster,' she said softly.

Bob gulped. The wily old sheriff had known who he was all the time.

'Dearest Bob, I wanted to tell you that we all knew who you had been, but Uncle Hal said I had to wait until you discovered who you had become.'

Becky grabbed hold of Bob possessively and kissed him.

'Now that you have, I think Pa had better get the priest, very quickly. I'm not going to wait much longer,' Becky said, looking shamelessly into Bob's eyes.

'Becky, shame on you. Come into the house this minute!' They had been too engrossed in each other to notice Mrs Lorimer as she approached. But in spite of her reproach she was smiling.

Arm-in-arm, Becky and Bob walked into the ranch house. They were greeted with the homely aroma of Mrs Lorimer's superb cooking. For the first time in his life, Bob felt he had a home.

Mrs Lorimer followed them. But before she went in, she picked up the unwanted boots and dropped them into the trash bin. The ghost of Bob's past, Jack Crow, had finally been laid to rest.

THE END